SOMETHING WICKED ...

"Keith, dear?" a creepy, high-pitched voice crackled over the phone. "There's a present for you and that darling family of yours. It's at your back door."

The line clicked dead.

Goosebumps lifted along Keith's arms. Slowly, he put down the phone. Then he called out toward the porch, "Wrong number, Mom."

There was one thing he was sure of—he didn't want the family to know whatever it was that waited outside in the dark . . .

THE PARTRIDGE FAMILY #5 TERROR BY NIGHT

BY VIC CRUME

CURTIS
BOOKS

MODERN LITERARY EDITIONS PUBLISHING COMPANY
NEW YORK, N.Y.

CAST OF CHARACTERS

THE PARTRIDGES—

Shirley Partridge—Is "Mom" to five talented children. When the Partridge Family is on tour, it's Shirley who's behind the wheel of the big bus painted in psychedelic colors. Her bright, strong singing voice has helped make the Partridge Family famous from coast to coast.

Keith Partridge—Shirley's oldest son is "man of the family." A great help to his widowed mother, Keith plays guitar for the group.

Laurie Partridge—Shirley is proud of her pretty teenage daughter. Laurie's singing is an important part of the Partridge fame.

Danny Partridge—Like his older brother, Danny is great on guitar, and at ten years old, he has a steel-trap mind for business.

Christopher Partridge—Is an eight-year-old winner on the drums. He keeps the beat for the group.

Tracy Partridge—Baby of the family, she gives the group plenty of singing support wherever the Partridge Family performs.

Shirley Partridge recorded a song in the family garage with her five talented children —and the family was destined for stardom from the first scratch of a needle! Now they travel in a renovated old school bus painted in bright psychedelic colors. Shirley drives them all over the country in search of life, liberty, and the pursuit of singing engagements.

REUBEN HAS A PLAN

☐ Keith Partridge leaned against the kitchen doorway and watched his mother expertly flip a golden-brown pancake on the smoking griddle.

"There's enough on the platter for a start," Shirley Partridge said. "Come on, Keith. Eat 'em while they're hot!"

"Not me!" Keith grinned.

Shirley looked at him in surprise. "What do you mean, not you?" she asked. "Keith, you feel all right, don't you?"

Keith laughed. "I feel great. But, Mom, just last night you gave us a lecture on how the family that plays together is going to begin eating together—or else! So I'm waiting for the others. Your orders."

At that moment, Danny and Christopher, the younger Partridge boys, came trooping into the kitchen. Close at their heels was Tracy, the baby of the family, with Simone, the Partridge Family poodle.

"Hi, kids," Shirley smiled. "Good morning."

"Pancakes, hey, great! Hi, Mom." And all three made a dash for the table.

Keith called out sternly, "Hold it, men. Wait for Laurie. Don't you remember Mom's speech last night on eating *together?*"

Luckily for everyone, Shirley's teenage daughter strolled into the kitchen just then.

"Mmm! Pancakes!" she exclaimed. "Hi, everybody."

As the breakfast chatter began, Shirley looked around at her talented bunch. They were hardworking, hard-playing, real kids. Not one was puffed with importance because they'd become almost a household word in thousands of American homes. The Partridge Family—one of the outstanding rock groups in the whole country!

Shirley sighed. "I should have planned a real vacation for them this summer," she thought. "The kids deserve it. They should see something new—go someplace where they'd make new friends and have fun."

Suddenly she sat up straight. "Well, why can't we have a vacation?" she asked herself. "We don't have a thing on the schedule until the rock concert Labor Day weekend in Massachusetts—and there's still half of August ahead."

"What's the matter, Mom? Something wrong?" Keith asked.

Shirley laughed. "Goodness, no! I was just thinking —how about our taking—"

The sharp ring of the telephone in the hallway interrupted her sentence. Keith pushed back his chair.

"I'll get it, Mom. Wonder who's calling so early in the morning?"

In a moment he called out from the hallway. "For you, Mom. It's Reuben Kinkaid."

"At this hour!" Shirley exclaimed, rising from her chair. "Now what on earth ever got our business manager out of bed this early in the morning? Laurie, you take over the next pancake batch, will you?" She hurried out of the kitchen.

Laurie stood over the smoking griddle. Cakes had been disappearing almost as fast as she poured the batter.

"Mom's been talking for *hours*," she said. "Talk about us monopolizing the phone!"

"Was it a person-to-person call, Laurie?" Danny asked.

"Why?" Laurie asked coldly. Sometimes Danny's money-conscious mind was very irritating to his older sister.

"I was merely thinking that if it's a person-to-person call, it means Mr. Kinkaid must be getting very rich as our business manager. Because person-to-person calls cost more than—"

"Oh, Danny. Stop it!"

"What's the matter, Laurie?" Keith grinned. "Can't you understand that when Danny programs his mighty brain, the answer just has to flip out?"

Laurie made a face. "Talking about money is crude!"

"Okay. So face it," Keith replied. "Danny is a crude computer."

At that point Shirley came back into the kitchen waving a sheet of paper in her hand. "What do you suppose!" she exclaimed happily. "Talk about two souls with but a single thought!"

"What?" asked the family together.

"Well, just when the phone rang, I was going to ask you how you'd feel about taking a vacation someplace, and that's exactly what Reuben called about! He said he'd been thinking we needed a vacation, but with the concert coming up he realized we'd need to do some rehearsing—and he's been trying to think of where we could vacation and rehearse, too."

"What's the problem?" Danny asked. "People could hear us for nothing if we were rehearsing at a summer place."

Shirley laughed. "This may come as quite a shock, Danny, but not everybody in the world enjoys rock practice right in the middle of a peace-and-quiet vacation."

She looked back at the others. "Anyhow, he's found just the spot for us—a big beach house. And it's right on the Atlantic Ocean. At least, the ocean is on one side and there's a quiet cove on the other. *And* Reuben has arranged for the owner's cook to stay on and cook for us. And that's not all—we're going to have the use of a station wagon, too. Doesn't it sound wonderful?"

"It *sounds* wonderful, Mom," Keith said, "but where is it? I mean, *where* along the Atlantic Ocean?"

Shirley looked at the crudely drawn map she had made. "It's in Massachusetts. But"—her face grew pink—"you won't believe this, kids, but all I've written down are highways numbers, the ones after we've passed Boston. I guess I was so thrilled about the beach house and the wagon and the cook and everything that I just forgot to ask Reuben the exact name of the place. I'll have to call him back."

Keith frowned. "But why would Reuben forget to

tell *you?* Honestly, Mom, I'll bet it's some dumpy place beyond the sound of a human voice, and he was just afraid to say so."

"When it comes to picking out places for us to stay, I absolutely don't trust Mr. Kinkaid, Mom," Laurie added. "I'll bet it's someplace nobody ever dreamed of going to, like—like—East Gooseberry or East Goosebump." Laurie giggled.

"Is it someplace where me and Danny can camp out and live off the land?" Chris asked.

"Why not?" Shirley answered. "We're going to have eight acres of privacy. And with a station wagon, Keith, I guess you and Laurie will be within range of people. So let's get in a real vacation mood, even if Reuben tells us that we are heading for East Goosebump!"

Once again at the telephone, Shirley thoughtfully set it back in its cradle. Keith had been right. Reuben *hadn't* wanted to tell them the exact place they were going.

Why on earth, of all the vacation spots along the Massachusetts shore, did Reuben have to pick out a place with the chilling name of Haunt Port?

"Oh, well!" she shrugged. "If it's a village, that means people live there." But just the same a quick shiver ran along her spine. Haunt Port! It sounded, well—sinister!

THE HANGING TREE

☐ Haunt Port—7 mi.

Shirley Partridge wheeled the big, wildly painted Partridge Family bus off the main highway and into a quiet winding road.

"What time is it, Keith?" she asked. "I forgot to wind my watch."

"Nearly seven," Keith answered. "And am I hungry!"

"When we pick up the beach house keys at Parsons' grocery store, they'll probably tell us where we can find a good restaurant," Shirley said. "I hope the store is still open. We'll have to find where the Parsons live, if it isn't."

She slowed the bus. "My goodness! Haunt Port is going to be private. It isn't even on this road. I nearly missed that sign."

A weathered wooden arrow pointed to the left. Haunt Port—1 mi. Shirley turned the bus into a narrow, winding road that began an uphill climb. At the top of the rise was a small sign as old and weathered as the pointed arrow they had nearly missed. It announced that they had arrived in Haunt Port—pop. 291, founded 1620.

"Population two hundred and ninety-one!" Keith exclaimed. "Gosh! It hasn't grown much."

"Mr. Kinkaid said it would be private," Danny piped up. "Man! We got us a private town!"

The bus rounded another curve and the village spread before them.

"This is more like it!" Shirley exclaimed. "How pretty!"

On either side of the road, neat little New England cottages sat square in the middle of grassy lawns. Lemon-yellow, weathered-silver, brown-shingled, or white, each had its flower-decked path leading to the road and to a mailbox. Just beyond, "downtown" Haunt Point lined either side of the sloping main street. And at its foot was the blue cove where small sailing boats swung at anchor, and fishing boats were tied at a wharf.

"Where are the people?" Laurie asked. "There isn't a soul in sight."

"All two hundred and ninety-one are having dinner," Keith answered.

"There's the store and it's open," Shirley said.

She pulled the big bus to the curb and stopped.

"Let's both go in, Keith," she said. "I want to pick up food for Simone."

As they stepped to the sidewalk, the clock in the church steeple was bonging the hour. It was exactly seven o'clock.

"That must be Mr. Parsons behind the counter," she said.

Keith followed as Shirley stepped quickly into the

store. But he hardly heard his mother greeting Mr. Parsons. His eyes were fastened on a denim- and jersey-clad girl. She was kneeling on the floor and stacking soup cans on the lowest shelf. When she raised a brown hand and swished back a pale-yellow curtain of long blond hair, two dark-lashed brown eyes looked up at him. As far as Keith Partridge was concerned, they belonged to the most beautiful girl he had ever seen.

"Hi," said this enchanting being.

"Hi," answered Keith.

"I've seen you on TV," she smiled. "You're Keith Partridge, aren't you?"

Keith cleared his throat. "Yes," he managed to say.

"I'm Jane Parsons."

"Oh, hi," Keith said again. "I'm Keith Partridge."

Jane Parsons grinned. "Hi."

Over at the counter, Shirley talked to Mr. Parsons. He kept glancing beyond her at the psychedelic paint job of the bus parked outside his store.

"Say!" he interrupted suddenly. "I just realized— you're the *famous* Partridge Family! Will Mrs. Parsons and Jane be pleased! I don't know why I didn't recognize you right off!"

Just then Mrs. Parsons came through the doorway behind the counter. She laughed and held out her hand.

"I heard that," she said. "It just goes to show we should have color TV. Welcome to Haunt Port, Mrs. Partridge."

"I should say so," her husband exclaimed. "Being Haunt Port's chief of police, I don't always have the chance to see your program, but I'll bet Jane knew you right off. She collects your records."

Shirley smiled. "Well, we're glad to be here, and it's nice to be welcome. You know, I was just telling the children that I imagined you could suggest a good restaurant to us. We're a pretty hungry bunch."

"Not a restaurant for twelve miles," Mrs. Parsons said. "But there's no need for you to make a drive like that, not if you like fresh chowder and blueberry pie. We sell both right here—sort of a sideline to the grocery."

Shirley hesitated.

"I'll tell you what, Mrs. Partridge," Mrs. Parsons said. "You take the house keys and go along now and I'll send Jane over in Mrs. Snow's station wagon with eats, if you folks will drive her back here again. That way you'll have the station wagon tonight and be all set for your vacation at Witch's Hollow."

"*Witch's Hollow?*" Shirley exclaimed. "What's that?"

Chief Parsons laughed. "Oh, that's just what Mrs. Snow's place is called hereabouts."

"My goodness—how does Mrs. Snow feel about *that?*"

"Oh, it's nothing to do with her," the chief said hastily. "It's been called Witch's Hollow for just about three hundred years. History, you might say."

He took a pencil from behind his ear and bent over a pad of sales slips. "Now this is the way to get there." He drew a little map. "See? It's ideal. You have the ocean in front and the cove waters on the south side. That's the beauty of Hangman's Hill!"

Shirley gasped. "What happened to Witch's Hollow?"

Chief Parsons chuckled. "It's all one and the same property. When the Snows bought it, they tried to get folks to change the name. But it just didn't catch on, and it's still called Hangman's Hill like it was long ago."

Shirley shook her head. "I hope we don't run into either one—witches or hangmen."

She turned to Keith. "Keith, Mrs. Parsons is sending our dinner over with—Oh! You must be Jane."

Jane scrambled to her feet, her brown eyes glowing with friendliness. "How'd you do," she grinned. "I was just telling Keith—I hope you'll let me come over and hear you practice. I just love—"

"Rock!" her mother and father said together.

Everybody laughed with everybody, and then the Partridges left the store.

Even though the sky was filled with soft evening light, big arching trees made a tunnel of gloom in the long lane that led to the beach house. Shirley looked ahead uneasily. "Hangman's Hill," she muttered to herself. "If this turns out to be one of Reuben Kinkaid's peculiar arrangements, I don't know what we'll do. I've spent all our vacation money."

Just then the big bus emerged from the leafy tunnel and there were cries of delight from everybody, and Shirley's uneasy feeling vanished. Straight ahead the Atlantic Ocean spread in a dark-blue band. On either side of a grassy meadow spangled with field flowers were dark pines and great gray boulders. And toward the right, almost on the edge of land and sea, a big two-story house towered against the sky. It would have looked dark and foreboding, but rambler roses climbed in huge tangles of crimson color between sparkling clean windows and on either side of a doorway.

"Oh boy, Dan—look at all this! We can camp out almost anywhere!" Chris cried out.

"Me, too!" Tracy squealed.

"Where's the cove?" Laurie asked.

"On the other side of those high rocks, I suppose," Keith answered. "Maybe we could rent a boat, Mom."

"Let's try," Shirley replied. She slowed the bus. "I don't see a garage and we'll want to keep the drive clear for the station wagon. How about parking under that huge old tree, Keith?"

"Right next to those big rocks would be better," Keith suggested. "Pull in close and it will be out of the way."

Tracy was the first to spot Jane Parsons as she came driving up the lane, and the entire family, including Simone, rushed out to greet her.

"Hi," she called out. "I guess you folks are starved. Mother and I decided we'd better make sandwiches to go along with the chowder, and it took longer." She climbed out of the station wagon and went around to lower the tailgate.

It wasn't long before the Partridges and Jane were seated around a long table set on the big screened porch facing the ocean. There were stacks of wonderful lobster sandwiches, steaming bowls of chowder, and two blueberry pies cut into juicy purple wedges.

"I guess you'll be eating out here a lot, Mrs. Partridge," Jane said politely. "It's a lovely view, isn't it?"

"What's that light way over there that keeps blinking?" Chris asked.

"Judbury Light. It's a lighthouse on the point across the cove," Jane replied. "And that reminds me—Dad said that heavy ground fog is predicted for tonight. So I guess if someone would drive me, it would be a good idea for me to go home now."

Shirley nodded. "That does sound like good sense. Keith, why don't you and Laurie go along with Jane and I'll get the rest of the family organized for the night. And—oh!—call Simone in before you go."

But for once the little poodle didn't come bounding up in answer to Keith's whistle.

"She'll probably be barking at the door before we're back," Keith said. "Let's get started."

Wisps of fog were already gently curving and swaying across the road as Keith headed the station wagon toward Haunt Port. And before they were a third of the distance there, fog filled every dip in the road with thick waving bands.

"Your dad was sure right," Keith said, slowing the car. "Does this happen every night up here?"

Jane laughed. "Not—"

"Oh!" Laurie cried out in horror. "Look!"

In the blurred beam of the headlights, a weird, gray figure loomed out of the low-lying fog. It was draped in a long cloak, and long black hair hung about its shoulders, and in its arms was a huge black cat, eyes blazing an electric green.

"My gosh!" Laurie exclaimed as they passed by the figure. "It is a *person*. I thought it was a witch."

There was a moment's silence. Then, in a dismal voice, Jane said, "I forgot to tell your mother about the cook."

"Don't tell us *that* was the cook!" Keith exclaimed.

Unexpectedly, Jane giggled. "No. That was Pru Judbury, the cook's daughter."

"Well, she's sure no ad for her mother's cooking," Keith said.

"I wonder what she was doing way out here," Jane said. "They live on the other side of Haunt Port. Oh, well—nobody knows what Pru Judbury does. She's pretty odd. But will you tell your mother that Mrs. Judbury will be at the beach house first thing in the morning? Mother will bring them out with their luggage and they'll use the housekeeper's rooms downstairs. And she is a good cook, even if Pru does look like, like—"

"A bewitched beanpole," Keith said gloomily. "And *living* with us!"

It was a slow drive back. Keith heaved a sigh of relief as they neared the end of the beach house drive.

Lighted upstairs windows showed that the younger Partridges still were not settled for the night. But at least they were in the house—and that was good. Only Keith heard Laurie's screams.

Up ahead, from the bough of the big old tree that Shirley had admired, a horrible, dark shape swung from the end of a rope. Slowly it turned, left . . . right . . . left . . . right . . . above the low-lying fog.

"Laurie, cut it out! Stop that yelling. It's nothing but a dummy, you idiot!"

Laurie held her hands over her eyes. "How . . . how do you know?" she asked in a shaking voice.

"Because I can see." He pulled the car close and stopped. "Come on, let's get it down. We don't want Mom and the kids to know about this. It would ruin Mom's vacation."

"Somebody wants to ruin it," Laurie said, close to tears.

"Aw, it's just kid stuff. Forget it."

But when Keith read the black letters scrawled across the sheet of paper pinned to the dummy, his blood chilled.

WELCOME! THE HANGMAN.

He stuffed the note in his pocket.

"I'll hide the dummy in the bus. You go in the house. And Laurie—*try* not to look so dismal."

One more thing was to mark that first night at the beach house—Simone did not come back. For the first time in a long time, the little poodle was not on guard beneath the Partridge Family roof.

THE WITCH'S DAUGHTER

☐ Keith Partridge woke up to the wonderful smell of sea air. The soft swish of waves on the rocks below reminded him that the first day of vacation was starting!

He flung back the covers and went to the window. It was a beautiful day—a day that wiped out the ugliness of last night's happening.

He hurried to shower, dress, and rush down to breakfast. But at the kitchen doorway he came to a sudden stop. The tallest, boniest woman he had ever seen was standing at the kitchen stove turning bacon in the frying pan. She glanced up—or down—at him.

"Good morning," Keith said. "I guess you're Mrs. Judbury." He held out his hand. "I'm Keith Partridge."

Mrs. Judbury ignored his hand. "Morning," she replied, her thin lips barely shaping a smile. "Do you eat now or do you wait for your folks?"

Remembering the last time the family had waited for each other, Keith hastily answered, "Now, please. But I can help myself."

"Sit down," Mrs. Judbury said. She plunked a plate of toast and bacon and eggs on the table. "I'll get the marmalade. Or do you want to try beach plum jam? It's famous around here."

There was the sound of the outside kitchen door opening. Keith looked up. Standing in the doorway was a tall, sharp-featured girl about his own age—the girl Keith had seen in the fog the night before. Smoky black hair hung straight below her shoulders, and in her sharp-elbowed, deeply tanned arms was a tremendous black cat. She glanced unsmilingly at Keith, then quickly looked away.

"Come in, Prudence," Mrs. Judbury said. "I see you have Benjamina."

The girl took one step forward and came to a dead halt. The cat leaped from her arms and marched over to Mrs. Judbury.

"Prudence, this is Keith Partridge. This is my daughter," she said to Keith.

Keith pushed back his chair and stood up. "I guess you're in time for coffee or something," he said politely.

"Prudence has long since had her breakfast," Mrs. Judbury said. She turned to her daughter. "Did you walk or sail?"

"Sailed," Prudence answered, wasting no words.

"That reminds me," Keith said. "I saw a boathouse from my bedroom window. Is there a boat there?"

Mrs. Judbury and her daughter exchanged glances.

"You'll find no boathouse nor boat, young man. That's just the old boarded-up Witch's Hollow cottage."

"Where does the witch live now?" Keith asked, grinning.

"If ever there was one, she's been dead about three hundred years," Mrs. Judbury replied, scowling.

There was a silence, then Keith said, "Did either of you happen to see a poodle that looked lost? Ours disappeared last night."

Mrs. Judbury shook her head. Prudence acted as if she hadn't heard. "I'm going out," she said, and promptly slammed the kitchen door behind her.

Keith watched her stride away. Jane Parsons was right—Prudence Judbury certainly was odd.

Before the others were downstairs, Keith had already started his investigation of the ocean's shoreline and had rounded the point of the cove. He saw a tiny sailboat bobbing at anchor a short distance out from shore. And when he came abreast of the dark little cottage he had seen from his window, he saw Prudence Judbury staring out over the water.

"Hi," Keith called, not too pleased to see her. He walked over and looked at the cottage.

"Say, that place looks like one of those old New England houses that have a date on them. You know—historical houses."

"It's historical all right," Prudence answered in a low voice. "Old as anything they show off in Salem."

"Salem? Oh—that's where they burned witches, wasn't it?"

"Hung them," Prudence said shortly.

"Oh? The custom seems to have caught on," Keith said.

"What do you mean?" Pru asked sharply.

Keith hesitated. Maybe it would be better not to mention the dummy to anyone. He didn't want his mother to find out about it; she'd worry. "Oh, nothing," he said.

Then he asked, "Why is this place called Witch's Hollow? Did some famous old witch live here?"

Instead of answering, Prudence suddenly swooped her hand to the ground. Her fingers closed over something.

"Witch-pet! See. I can do it every time!" she exclaimed.

She opened her fingers, and there, standing on the palm of her hand, was a small, bumpy brown toad. It speedily hopped off and into the rough grass.

"What did you do that for?" Keith asked. "You must have scared him to death."

"He didn't look dead to me," Prudence replied calmly. "He hopped away pretty fast." She looked toward the path that led up to the rocks. "Who are they?" she asked.

Chris, Danny, and Tracy came jumping down the path and immediately began calling out excitedly.

"Are you Pru?" little Tracy asked.

For the first time Prudence Judbury smiled. Her face lit up, and her sharp features seemed to soften.

"I'm Pru. And who are you? And that's a poem," she laughed.

"Will you take us out in your boat, Pru?" Danny asked.

Keith spoke hastily. "Pru's boat is too small for a bunch like us. Mom said maybe she'd rent a boat more our size."

"We could go in Pru's boat one at a time," Chris suggested.

"She'd love that," Keith grinned. "You wait for Mom to get a boat. Besides, I thought you were going to live off the land and go camping."

"We are. We're going to camp right down here," Chris said. "Will you help us, Keith?"

Prudence shivered. "I wouldn't camp here next to —" She suddenly stopped, then said, "so close to open water."

Keith was sure she had started to say something else. "The kids could pitch their tent farther back from shore," he said.

Prudence shrugged. "Suit yourself," she said. And without another word, she began climbing the rocky path to the house.

"Say, Keith. I almost forgot—Mom wants you to go to the village for groceries," Danny piped up.

Keith watched Pru as she climbed up and over the rocks. "What a weird girl," he thought. But what he said, was, "Okay, Danny."

Jane was in sole charge of the store when Keith walked in. He waved his mother's long list. "Here it is. Stuff for the week—excepting what they've forgotten," he said.

Jane looked at it. "Whew! It'll take me more than just a second to get *this* together." She looked up. "Did your dog come home?"

Keith shook his head. "No. And something's happened I want to tell you about. Last—"

The screened door slammed and Keith turned to

see a tall, deeply tanned man enter the store. Jane called out, "Hello, Mr. Beresford. Back from New York City already?"

"Came in last night, and not a thing to eat in the house." He glanced at Keith.

"You're just in time to meet one of your new neighbors—you know, the family we told you about who rented the Snow place. Keith Partridge, Mr. Beresford."

Keith smiled and reached out his hand. Mr. Beresford touched it limply, and a look of dislike came and went swiftly across his handsome face. "Oh? That's fine," he said coldly. "How do your parents like it?"

"My father isn't living, sir," Keith replied with dignity. "But my mother and my two sisters and my two little brothers are having a great time. Then Mrs. Judbury and her daughter are with us, too. So we're quite a bunch."

This time Keith knew he wasn't imagining the mean look in Mr. Beresford's eyes. They glinted in displeasure, and he laughed unpleasantly. "Oh, I heard you were going to be stuck with the Judburys—the village witch and her weird witch daughter. Poor you!"

He turned away and said, "Jane, I'm in a hurry. I haven't had breakfast and I'm hungry. How about bread, coffee, eggs, bacon, and some oranges?"

Jane hesitated. She hadn't even begun the Partridge order.

"Go ahead, Jane," Keith said. "That's all right, I'll wait."

It didn't take Jane long to get Mr. Beresford's

supplies together and then, without so much as a thank you, he strode out the door.

Keith watched him cross the street, stow the sack of groceries into a long, low sports car.

"Who is he, besides being our neighbor?" Keith asked.

"Just about Haunt Port's most important summer visitor," Jane answered.

"Why? How so?" Keith asked.

"He's awfully rich, I guess. He has a big cruiser and a speed boat, too. And his house—it's full of art treasures! At least that's what everybody says. You know, he's a collector—he's been all over the world."

"No," Keith said. "I didn't know. What does he collect?"

"Priceless art treasures, naturally," Jane answered.

Keith growled. "He sure has priceless manners!" He turned to look at Jane. "Jane, how come you let him get away with calling Mrs. Judbury and her daughter witches? Man! I wouldn't let him talk that way about even my one hundred and ninetieth cousin!"

Jane flushed. "Well, I can't help what I can't help. They act pretty odd, both of them."

"But why did he call them witches?" Keith demanded.

Jane bent over the grocery list. "Why don't you look around the village while I get this together?" she suggested, ignoring the question.

Keith wanted to ask more, but Jane looked pretty angry. He thought a second. Things weren't going the way he had hoped.

"Okay. Let's drop it. Didn't you start to say something last night about selling tickets for a clambake you are having?"

"*I'm* not having it," Jane replied frostily. "The village of Haunt Port is raising funds for our returning Vietnam vets."

Keith's eyes widened. "Gosh, you can't have too many from a little town like Haunt Port, can you?"

"Two. And they're going to need money to get started again," Jane said. "How many tickets would you like, if any?"

"Six—no, eight," Keith answered.

"Eight!" Jane exclaimed. "Oh—counting the Judburys?"

"Anything wrong with that? After all, they're both going to be staying at the beach house and they're Haunt Port citizens, aren't they? Who knows? Maybe Pru might improve if she'd rub elbows with the human race."

"Oh, come on, Keith. Save your money. They won't go. Pru hates Haunt Port."

"Why?"

Jane shrugged. "Ask her."

Silently, she began stacking the groceries.

Keith kicked himself all the way back to Witch's Hollow. "How'd I ever get into this?" he groaned. "A great girl like Jane Parsons and I have to stick up for that—that toad catcher."

He was almost home when he suddenly remembered he hadn't said a word to Jane about the hanging dummy he and Laurie had hidden away.

"Oh, well—what could she do about it?" he said to himself. "It was only somebody's dumb joke anyhow, wasn't it?"

NO ANSWERS

□ After Keith had put the groceries in the kitchen, he went down to the cove to help Chris and Danny pitch the tent.

They had hardly started the job when Mr. Beresford, Shirley, and Laurie came down the path. Keith's mother was smiling, and Laurie gazed adoringly at Mr. Beresford.

"Here we go again," Keith thought. "Laurie has found another great new love."

It was Shirley's and Laurie's first glimpse of the old cottage.

"What a darling house!" Shirley exclaimed. "I wonder why Mrs. Snow doesn't keep it in repair."

"Now that's a very interesting story, Mrs. Partridge," Mr. Beresford said. "As I understand it, when the Snows bought this property from the Judbury family, it was written into the contract that the cottage would not be repaired, torn down, nor used, or it would revert to the former owners."

"How strange!" Shirley said.

"Well, *somebody* uses it," Laurie spoke up. "Look

at the path to the door. Somebody's whacked down all the brown-eyed Susans, and it's all trampled there."

Keith stared. "Now why didn't I notice that! Laurie's right," he thought.

Mr. Beresford laughed. "You have the makings of a detective, Laurie. But I imagine the answer is not very exciting. That doorstep is probably a handy place to sit down, lean back, and just look at the view. As you can see, the entrance is firmly boarded up."

Beresford was taking a lot of trouble to explain why a few flowers were crushed and trampled, thought Keith.

"Mr. Beresford," Danny asked, "have you seen Simone?"

"Simone?" Mr. Beresford smiled. "Have I missed meeting a member of the Partridge Family?"

"She certainly is a member," Shirley said. "She's our little dog, and she's disappeared."

"Maybe in a strange place she started for home," Mr. Beresford said. "Or maybe some passerby picked her up along the highway. Poodles are quite valuable, you know."

Keith glanced at Mr. Beresford and frowned.

"Oh, I think she's just having a little vacation of her own," Shirley said quickly, as she saw Tracy's face getting all set to cry.

Mr. Beresford glanced at his watch. "Goodness! I know I'm keeping you people from lunch. Time flies!" He paused, looked over at the old cottage and said, "You know, you people ought to take time to visit Salem if you haven't been there. It has quite a witch history, you know. And if I remember correctly, that cottage is somehow connected with it."

"Witches!" Chris and Danny called out. They jumped to their feet and rushed over to the group. "Tell us," they demanded.

Mr. Beresford gave a short laugh. "Ask your cook and her daughter. They probably know more on that subject than most people." He looked at the cottage again. "So you're camping right here, boys?"

"Isn't it a great spot!" Danny exclaimed.

Mr. Beresford turned toward the path. "I don't know about that. Personally, *I* wouldn't camp here for anything."

"Why?" Shirley said. "What do you mean?"

Mr. Beresford's dark eyes gleamed. He smiled and looked apologetic. "Probably I shouldn't have said it, Mrs. Partridge. It's just that—well, I'm afraid witches are on my mind when I'm around here."

He turned toward the rocks, then looked back. "—or hangmen," he added. "Gloomy, isn't it?"

Keith was last up the path. He looked up at the back of Mr. Beresford's shining, dark head, and an uneasy thought nibbled at the back of his mind. Mr. Beresford had said something odd, some one thing, and Keith wished he could remember. What was it? He turned back and looked down at the old cottage. For some reason, even in the bright noonday sun, it looked dark and—sinister.

Mrs. Judbury had hamburgers broiling in the oven when the family trooped up for lunch. She nodded toward the trays stacked on the kitchen table. "This is a help-yourself lunch, folks. Get your plates ready. These burgers are about done."

"Where's Pru?" Laurie asked, stabbing at a pickle and putting it on Tracy's tray.

"Here," Pru answered, opening the screened door.

"Why didn't you come down to the cove with us, Pru? Mr. Beresford is *so* interesting. And that darling cottage! He was telling us—" Laurie stopped as Pru rudely turned her back.

Keith hurriedly spoke up. "Among other things, he was telling us he wouldn't set up camp down there in the cove. He seems to agree with Pru. What's all this mystery about the cove, anyhow?"

"Yeah," Danny said. "All that stuff about witches! Does Mr. Beresford think we're babies or something?"

Pru and her mother exchanged quick glances, but not quick enough that Keith and Laurie didn't notice.

Tracy, her hamburger in hand, looked round-eyed at everybody. "Witches?" she asked. "Where're the witches?"

"Where's the best swimming beach? Ours looks pretty muddy," Shirley said quickly.

Pru turned and nodded. "Only way to swim around here is to dive off a boat. But there's a good sandy, sloping beach farther in along the cove."

"How far?" Shirley asked.

"Oh, about—I don't know—about a five-minute walk along the shore, I guess."

Shirley thought a minute. "Why don't we all pitch in after lunch and help the boys bring their gear back over on this side of the rocks, then all go swimming?" she suggested.

"Aw, Mom!" Chris and Danny exploded together.

"Gosh, Mom, are *you* afraid of witches?" Danny asked.

"I'm afraid of that climb over the rocks in the dead of night," Shirley said, "if anyone had a stomach ache, or something, and wanted to come back to the house."

Chris looked up in surprise. "Who has stomach aches?"

"I have an idea," Mrs. Judbury said. "Why don't you boys pitch your tent right by the path on this side? Then you'd be handy to the cove in case you'd like to cook your breakfast down there. I believe I could spare a frying pan, and you could take provisions for a hearty meal."

Chris and Danny looked at each other. "Well," Chris said slowly, "I guess that would be okay. How about you, Dan?"

Danny nodded. His eyes twinkled. "Sure. I guess so. Anything—just so's we can camp out."

From the little beach, Keith watched Pru helping Tracy to improve her dog-paddle stroke. Pru, wearing a pale-green swimsuit, looked like a tanned, smoky-haired mermaid.

Shirley noticed Keith frowning thoughtfully. "What's worrying you, if anything?" she asked.

"Not much. I was just wondering if Pru's father was a midget."

Shirley sat up. "A what?"

"Well, Mrs. Judbury's extra tall. If Mr. Judbury was her size, it seems to me that Pru would be way over the average."

"She's certainly way over the average when it comes to swimming," Shirley said.

"Mom," Keith said, slowly, "do you believe in witches? Do you?"

"Witches! Keith, you don't suppose you've been out in the sun too long? What is this—midgets, witches—anyhow?"

Keith jumped up, "Let's swim," he said, laughing.

Luckily for Shirley Partridge, she couldn't hear the conversation between Chris and Danny out in the water.

"Just one thing, Dan," Chris said in a low voice. "We've got to be *very* careful that they don't see us go down to the cove tonight. We don't want to spoil Mom's vacation. That stuff about stomach aches didn't fool me. Mom's scared of witches."

Danny nodded. "Yeah. And if she sees us, she'll spoil our vacation. Man, Chris! This is the best place we've ever been to!"

When the family returned to the beach house, Mrs. Judbury was shelling peas for dinner and listening to the radio.

"What people won't think of next," Mrs. Judbury said, reaching over and turning off the set. "Now who'd think any self-respecting millionaire would buy art stolen from a church?"

"Where did that happen?" asked Shirley.

"Italy," Mrs. Judbury replied. "I sometimes think the whole world's gone mad."

"Gone sad is more like it," Laurie said dramatically. "Why can't people just be decent to each other?"

"Hey! That reminds me," Keith exclaimed. "They're having a clambake in Haunt Port to raise money for returning Vietnam vets. I bought tickets for all of us."

He turned to Mrs. Judbury. "We'll be counting on you and Pru to steer us around, Mrs. Judbury. We don't know one end of a clam from another."

Pru and her mother looked quickly at each other, and Pru shook her head the least bit.

"It's a worthy cause and one we'd want to contribute to, Keith," Mrs. Judbury said. "Pru, get my purse, will you?"

As Pru left the room, Mrs. Judbury said, "Pru and I aren't much of ones for social doings, but I'm sure the Parsons will see to it that you don't eat the shells and throw away the clams."

"You mean you won't go?" Shirley asked in surprise.

Mrs. Judbury nodded. "But thank you just the same," she said.

Shirley looked puzzled. No member of the Partridge Family ever turned down a chance for fun— and certainly a clambake sounded like fun.

"Maybe you'll change your minds," she said politely. "We all hope you will."

"All but me," Keith almost said aloud. "For all I care, Pru Judbury can stay home and cast spells. That's probably *her* idea of a real blast."

STORM AT THE COVE

☐ Even in the dark it was not too hard to find the beach house telephone line. It led from the roof line down along a corner wall. The dark figure standing in the deep shadows reached out to cut it through, and right away stuck all ten fingers on the thorny crimson ramblers.

At that same instant the kitchen lights went on and through the open window came a quick glimpse of two girls walking into the kitchen. Hastily, the intruder ducked down into raking thorns.

"Hey, who said 'ouch'?" one voice asked.

"I thought you had," another voice replied. "I was just going to ask you what was wrong."

"Guess we heard a night bird," the first voice replied.

There was no time to lose—a quick snip, the telephone wire was cut, and the dark figure hurried off in the black night.

In the kitchen, Laurie took the milk from the refrigerator as Pru reached into a cupboard for the can of cocoa.

"Honestly," Laurie said, pouring milk into a sauce-pan. "When we first came, I really didn't think I was going to like this place. But I'm changing my mind. Maybe it's because you and your mother are being so nice to us."

Pru looked down at her hands. "We're not that popular with most people."

Laurie hesitated. "I don't see how you can be popular, or unpopular either, if you never go anywhere. What do you have against people, anyhow?"

Pru spooned out the cocoa. "As far as I'm concerned, people can—"

"Where's that cocoa I've been hearing about?" Keith asked, coming in just then.

"Give us time," Laurie said. "Reach down the cups and saucers, will you, Keith?"

"Keith . . ." Shirley came to the door. "Mrs. Judbury thinks a storm might be blowing up. It's been lightning over the ocean and an east wind has sprung up."

"So you want me to rescue the sleeping beauties. Is that it?" Keith asked, lifting a stack of saucers from the shelf. "Right this minute?"

"Well, you know how Danny hates thunder."

"Gosh, Mom! What do you think pioneer kids did out there on the prairie in a covered wagon?"

"Stayed in the wagon with the rest of the family, I suppose," Shirley said calmly. Then she suddenly clapped a hand to her face. "Oh! I've forgotten to call Reuben. I meant to ask him before we left if he'd have our new costumes sent up here." She hurried off.

"Reuben is our business manager. Reuben Kinkaid," Laurie said to Pru. "We don't know what we'd do without him. I'll bet he'll bring our costumes up himself, don't you, Keith?"

The cocoa hadn't even begun to simmer when Shirley came back. "Now what do you suppose? The phone's dead."

"Are you sure it was connected, Mom?" Keith asked.

"Yes. It was working all right this afternoon. I called Mrs. Parsons to put in another order for chowder," Shirley replied.

"If you have to call Reuben tonight," Keith offered, "I could drive you to Haunt Port. There's a public phone there."

"Oh, it isn't that important. I'll try later."

A sudden flash of lightning turned the scene outside a livid blue-white, but the roll of thunder that followed was still far away. Shirley looked hard at Keith, who started toward the outside door. "Don't drink all the cocoa, girls." He grinned. "I'll be right back."

As he stepped beyond the light thrown by the kitchen windows, the night was solid black. "What I need is a flashlight," Keith thought. "The kids have the only one."

Just then the kitchen door banged. He looked back and saw Pru against the light of the doorway.

"Keith?" she called.

"Over here," he answered, then walked back toward the light.

Pru hurried. "I know the grounds," she said, shortly. "I'll go with you."

With Pru's sense of direction plus one revealing flash of lightning, it didn't take long to reach the tent.

Keith fumbled in the dark for the tent flap. "Chris! Danny!" he called.

His hand touched the flap. It was dangling loosely, and he flung it back. "Hey, Chris—wake up!" He ducked down, stepped inside, and listened. There was not a sound. Kneeling down, he patted his hand around trying to locate the bedrolls. He found the bedrolls—but no boys.

"Those kids!" He backed out of the tent. "I've a pretty good idea where they are," he said disgustedly.

"Down in the cove?" Pru asked.

"Where else? Why sleep in a nice tent when you can have a wild time waiting for a witch to show up in Witch's Hollow!"

There was an angry mutter from Pru. "That's what you get for telling them nonsense about witches," she snapped. "Find your own brothers—or or get Jane Parsons to help you. *She's* probably told you all about the Judbury witches." She turned back to the beach house.

"Wait!" Keith strode after her angrily.

Pru stopped. "Well?"

"Don't worry. I can 'find my own brothers.' But get something straight—Jane Parsons isn't talking about Judbury witches or any other witches, either!"

"Oh, no?" Pru snapped. "I'll *bet*."

A flash of lightning seemed to turn night to day, and for an instant, Keith saw her face. It was ugly with anger—or was it fear?

There was an enormous clap of thunder. Then, as it died, Pru spoke in a hard voice, "Come on. Let's hurry."

She silently and swiftly led the way to the rock

path, and close behind her Keith staggered and stumbled on the steep, rocky ground.

"Hey, Pru, slow down," he said. "We don't want to suddenly step on them."

"That's not likely; I haven't changed them into toads!" Pru exclaimed, then burst into a wild, shrill laugh.

Their backs pressed tight against the boarded-up door of Witch's Hollow cottage, Chris and Danny sat close together and stared into the dark.

"Hear it, Danny?" Chris whispered. "There *is* somebody coming!" His voice shook.

There was another rattle of sliding pebbles along the path above them.

"It's just some animal," Danny whispered back. "What'd you expect in the wilds anyhow?" he added crossly.

"The witch!" Chris chattered back, grabbing for Danny's arm.

"Next time I go camping with *you*—" Danny began scornfully.

Then from high on the path came the sound of wild laughter. Chris clutched at Danny. "The witch's cackle!" He gasped.

Now sounds of footsteps were unmistakable. And they were coming closer, *closer*. "There's two of them!" Danny gulped. The boys clung together, their hearts bumping against their ribs.

"Chris! Danny! Where are you guys?"

"It's Keith!" the two boys gasped in relief. They jumped up.

"Better stay where you are," Danny shouted, suddenly brave. "It's pretty dangerous for somebody who doesn't know their way around down here."

Keith snorted. "Then how about helping me find my way back?" he called.

"Okay. We'll give you a hand," Danny grandly offered.

In the next flash of lightning, Pru and Keith saw both the campers come to a skidding stop and cover their ears with their hands—and just in time! Thunder shook Witch's Hollow, and one flash of lightning followed another. In the sharp glare, Pru leaped quickly down the path to the boys.

"Indian file—and hurry. It's going to come pouring down any second."

Pru was right. Homeward bound, they were drenched.

In bed, Keith listened to the pound of surf on the rocks below. The storm had passed to the west but there were still distant rolls of thunder.

He punched his pillow. "Man!" he breathed. "If Mr. Beresford's ever seen Pru the way I saw her tonight, I couldn't blame him for calling her a witch. There's something wrong with that girl. I wonder why Laurie likes her."

He thought a minute. "But even if she was out on the road last night, that doesn't mean she hung a dummy from the tree. But she could have. She could have had it hidden somewhere, and then strung it up."

He turned over. "But why would she do it? No. Toads. I guess toads would be more her thing."

MR. BERESFORD'S INVITATION

☐ Shirley Partridge came into the kitchen. "Good morning, everybody," she said as she sat down.

"Oh, Keith—I'll take you up on the offer to drive into Haunt Port before we leave for Salem."

"Will you? I just tried the phone, and the line's still dead."

"Sure. Anybody want to come along?"

"I'll go," Laurie said. "I'd like to say hello to Jane Parsons."

Keith glanced at Pru, who had quickly looked down at her plate at the mention of Jane.

"Okay," he said, pushing back his chair. "Anytime you're ready." He stood up.

It was a beautiful fresh morning outside. Keith stopped to admire the crimson ramblers, still bright with sparkling raindrops from the previous night's rain.

Then his eyes caught something besides raindrops glinting in the morning sun. And it was something not beautiful at all, but dark and chilling—the frayed, cut ends of the black insulated telephone wire.

Laurie called out from the kitchen doorway. "Okay, I'm ready."

Keith turned and followed Laurie to the station wagon.

"Whew! It is hot in here," she exclaimed, rolling down the window. "Keith, are you in a trance or something? Lower your window, please."

"Sure." Keith headed the wagon down the drive. He frowned. "Laurie, which would you rather do— leave here or find out who hung the dummy and maybe stole Simone—and cut our telephone line?"

"Cut our telephone line!"

Keith nodded. "I just discovered it. And if Mom finds out, our vacation may end before it begins."

Laurie nodded. "If she'd known about that dummy, she'd have had us packed and in the bus in about two minutes flat."

"Maybe you'd just as soon leave," Keith said.

Laurie shook her head. "We'd never get Simone then," she said. "And I'm just sure she'll come back. Besides, I'm not scared—I mean not right now. I'm mad!"

"That's how I feel," Keith replied. "I want to find out *why* and I want to find out *who*."

"But Mom's bound to find out about the phone. The repairman would probably mention it. I don't imagine too many people get their line cut in two," Laurie said.

"Maybe Chief Parsons would help us out," Keith said. "You know, with the telephone company, bring official pressure to bear. If he could get them to send out a repairman today while we're in Salem, then Mom wouldn't need to know anything about it."

"Good idea," Laurie agreed. "Maybe Jane would help us—get her dad sort of on our side, I mean."

"Good morning!" Mrs. Parsons said cheerfully as the two Partridges came into the store. "What can I do for you?"

"We're just looking for Jane," Laurie said, smiling. "Is she around anywhere?"

"Over on the wharf," Mrs. Parsons replied. "She's helping her Dad shine up the *Lavinia Jane II*."

Jane Parsons, clad in faded-blue raggedy shorts and wearing a turned-down sailor hat, kneeled over a can of varnish.

"Hi, down there," Keith and Laurie called from the dock.

Jane looked up. "Oh, hi," she said, trying to look frostily at Keith and warmly at Laurie at the same time.

"Is your dad around?" Keith asked.

Chief Parsons just then emerged from the *Lavinia Jane II* cabin. "Hello, there," he greeted them, wiping his hands on a grease rag.

"You look pretty busy, sir," Keith said.

The chief chuckled. "You bet I am," he replied. "I'm supposed to be over at the town hall right this minute. I'm thinking of running for sheriff in the coming fall elections, you know."

A sudden idea leaped into Keith's mind. "Maybe if

you're going to run for sheriff what I want to tell you might be of extra interest, Chief—your being interested in crime, I mean—"

Chief Parsons laughed. "According to Jane, if I solved what's happened to your poodle, I'd probably win by a landslide in November. What's wrong?"

Jane had turned pink and was looking down at her varnish brush.

"This time it's our telephone line. It's been cut," Keith said.

"Your phone line cut! Well, why didn't you say so?"

Keith told him about how he had just happened to notice the wire. "We were just wondering if you could help us out in getting the phone company to fix it right away. We're going to be in Salem, and if the line was working when we got home, then Mother wouldn't need to know what happened. It would worry her a lot, you know."

Chief Parsons shook his head. "Oh, I can help you all right in having the line fixed right away," he said. "But this sounds as though a pretty ugly character is running around loose. I don't see not letting your mother know what's going on. Wouldn't be right."

Laurie groaned. "Well, good-bye Haunt Port! There goes our vacation, Chief Parsons."

"And there goes the whole case, if there is one. There must be *some* reason somebody doesn't want us here," Keith added. "If we let ourselves be scared off, nobody will ever know what *was* really going on."

Chief Parsons rubbed his chin. "Tell you what, Keith. If there is any more of this funny business, I'll put it fair and square to Mrs. Partridge. You know, it isn't as though Haunt Port can offer round-the-clock police protection to anybody. So far, what's happened is mean mischief, but I aim to not let it get out of hand. Understand?"

Keith nodded.

The chief glanced at his watch. "I'd better be getting along. Don't worry about your telephone. I'll take care of it. But don't you kids count on me keeping this a secret."

With those words he strode off, leaving two gloomy members of the Partridge Family with Jane.

Jane sighed. "I had a feeling things would end this way. Dad will do what he thinks is right."

"Oh, well—maybe nothing more will happen," Laurie said.

"If we don't get started for Salem, something is going to happen." Keith laughed. "We'll call you later, Jane."

"Keith," Laurie said, "let's not go. Let's look for clues or something, and *think*."

Jane looked puzzled. "I don't see how a cut telephone line could show much of a clue," she said.

"Footprints," Laurie answered. "Besides, we haven't really looked at the dummy since Keith put it in the bus."

"Dummy!" Jane exclaimed.

They told her about what had happened with the dummy.

"Well, don't tell Dad is all I can say."

Mr. Beresford's car was parked in the drive when Keith and Laurie arrived at the beach house.

"My day is ruined," Keith groaned, getting out of

the station wagon and giving the door an extra hard slam.

"I don't understand why you act so funny about Mr. Beresford," Laurie answered in a low voice. "At least, Keith, *try* to be polite." She hurried ahead of him toward the door.

At that moment Shirley Partridge and Mr. Beresford stepped out. "Good morning," Mr. Beresford said cheerfully. "I was just telling your mother that I'd tried to telephone but your line was dead."

"Did the phone company say they'd repair it today, Keith?"

Keith nodded. "They'll have it working before we're back from Salem."

"Mr. Beresford has just invited your mother to a party at his home tomorrow evening," Shirley said, smiling. "And invited us all to go out with him on his boat soon."

"I've explained that boats being what they are I can't invite all the Partridges at one time to go cruising in the *Estrelita* with me," Mr. Beresford said. "And so it's been decided that we'll make junior and senior expeditions, and you people work it out as you like. Perhaps Jane Parsons would like to join us on the 'senior' cruise. We could have lunch aboard."

"Oh, *wonderful!*" Laurie exclaimed, her eyes shining with pleasure. "That's certainly terribly nice of you, Mr. Beresford."

"Well, we'll plan on it." He smiled. "By the way— no more trouble around here I hope? It rather worried me when I learned your phone wasn't working."

Shirley laughed. "I guess the storm knocked it out."

"Thank goodness," Keith thought. "Mom's forgotten the line was dead *before* the storm!"

But Mr. Beresford said, "That's funny. Mine wasn't." He hesitated. "But you have had such bad luck here. First your dog is missing, then you find—er, your telephone out of order. Do you think your bus is safe?"

"I think our bad luck is over," Keith said easily.

"Oh?" Mr. Beresford's eyebrows went up.

"At least, we won't find the bus is missing or the tires slashed."

"What do you mean?" Mr. Beresford asked.

Keith grinned. "With that kind of bad luck, we couldn't leave."

"That's right!" Mr. Beresford exclaimed, an odd note of surprise in his voice. "I never thought of that. Well, I mustn't hold you up." He touched his cap to Shirley and stepped into his car.

"Have a fine time in Salem," he called back as he started down the drive. "Don't let the witches get you!"

Keith turned to Shirley. "Speaking of Salem, Mom—do you mind if Laurie and I don't go? We thought we'd like to just stay around here."

Shirley smiled. "Well, that's what a vacation is for —doing what you'd most like. We'll tell you all about Salem tonight."

WITCH'S HOLLOW

☐ Excepting Pru, who stalked off to her room, all of the Salem visitors were in high spirits upon their return. And so were Keith and Laurie. No horrible thing had happened at the beach house, the telephone line had been repaired, and the dummy was hidden in Laurie's closet as future possible "evidence."

"There was just one thing wrong," Danny sighed. "The witches in Salem weren't witches at all. Twenty people were hung and it was all a big mistake."

"And Pru wouldn't go into the Witch House with us," Tracy added.

"But the House of the Seven Gables was great!" Chris exclaimed. "You should have seen the secret staircase, Keith. I sure wish we had one."

Pru didn't appear at dinner time. Mrs. Judbury explained that her daughter had decided to go into Haunt Port on foot.

"Keith would have been glad to drive her," Shirley said.

"Thank you," Mrs. Judbury replied. "But Pru is an

independent sort of girl and likes to go her own way. Besides, the Haunt Port library is open tonight."

After the younger Partridges were off to bed, Mrs. Judbury settled herself on the porch, knitting bag in her lap. "Now don't you worry about those costumes, Mrs. Partridge," she said. "I shouldn't be a bit surprised if Mr. Kinkaid telephoned here inside of the next ten minutes to tell you all about it."

Shirley sighed. "I won't count on that. I'll just have to keep trying to reach him at his home number later this evening."

As she stopped talking, the telephone rang.

"Mr. Kinkaid," Mrs. Judbury said calmly.

"Probably Jane Parsons." Shirley laughed. "Keith, will you get it?"

Keith was back from the phone immediately. A surprised look was on his face. "It is Reuben, Mom," he said.

"No!" Shirley jumped up. "Mrs. Judbury, how on earth did you guess?" She rushed off to the phone.

Mrs. Judbury took out a ball of bright-orange yarn. "I'm knitting a winter comfy for Benjamina," she announced. "If there's anything that cat likes, it's some nice pully wool to curl up on of a chilly night."

"Orange is a lovely color for Benjamina," Laurie said, looking at the cat's velvety black profile. "It's sort of Halloweenish, isn't it?"

Mrs. Judbury nodded. "The very color for a witch's cat," she said calmly. "And, of course, anybody who's been in Haunt Port twelve hours—or maybe twelve minutes, for all I know—has heard Increase Judbury and her daughter are witches. Yes?" She looked over her spectacles at Keith and Laurie.

Laurie looked surprised, but Keith's face reddened. "What do you mean, Mrs. Judbury?" he asked.

Mrs. Judbury's needles clicked. "Oh, now Keith. Don't tell me you haven't heard that. If you do, I'll not believe it."

Shirley was smiling happily when she came back to the porch. "Everything is all set, kids," she said. "Reuben is coming up this weekend instead of next. We'll meet him at the airport in Boston. Isn't he a darling!"

She turned to Mrs. Judbury. "We don't know how we'd ever get along without Reuben, Mrs. Judbury. Not only is he our business manager, but he fusses over us like a—like a father hen!"

Mrs. Judbury suddenly dropped a stitch. "Well, I'll be pleased to meet him," she said. "I've yet to meet a father hen."

Shirley sat down. "Of course, you know what he asked, don't you?" she said to Keith and Laurie. " 'Have you been practicing'?"

Keith grinned. "And you had to tell him 'no,' when we'd been here for two whole days! But okay. Tomorrow morning we'll raise Mr. Beresford right through his roof."

Shirley frowned. "We can't even see his house from here, even if he is our closest neighbor. I don't think we'd bother him," she said. "Do you, Mrs. Judbury?"

Mrs. Judbury considered. "You might. He's north of us, and on a prevailing breeze you'd blow his way."

The Partridges burst out laughing.

"I guess I really feel like Christopher," Shirley said. "When we rehearse, people can hear us for free."

Just then there was a long, rumbling roll of thunder over in the east. "Not again!" Shirley groaned. "Do you suppose we're in for another thunderstorm? I hope it won't knock out our phone for the second night in a row."

Mrs. Judbury looked sharply at Keith. "I wouldn't worry about that. Would you, Keith?"

But before he could even wonder if Mrs. Judbury had known all along that the telephone line had been cut, she put down her knitting and said, "Now I recollect that you folks wanted to hear how this place got the names of Witch's Hollow and Hangman's Hill."

"Oh, yes!" Laurie said enthusiastically. "Mother said you'd promised to tell us."

Mrs. Judbury stuck her knitting needles into the ball of yarn and put them into the knitting bag. Benjamina leaped up and settled into her lap as a low peal of thunder grumbled out over the ocean.

"Well, Laurie, you and Keith missed it, but the others heard this afternoon how up Salem way about three hundred years ago they took a notion that witches were abroad in the land. At least twenty innocent folks were hung—or worse—before a judge whose head was set square on his shoulders put a stop to it all.

"Anyhow, one of my husband's Judbury ancestors had settled in Salem. And he hollered as loud as anybody about how spells had been put on people, and how all witches should be hung. Then after all the witch trouble in Salem came to an end, he moved away and came here to Haunt Port where his brother lived—Judburyport it was in those days. Maybe the thought of all those poor souls he helped send to their deaths was too much for him. I don't know. But I do know what happened next.

"He built himself and his wife that cottage down there in the hollow by the cove."

Mrs. Judbury paused and stroked Benjamina's sleek fur, then went on:

"But feelings ran so strong against the witch hangings in Salem that even his own brother in Judburyport turned against him; townsfolk began calling him 'the hangman.'

"He must have had a miserable life, because one day he marched up over the rocks and hung himself from that big tree you can see today by the drive."

"*That* tree!" Laurie gasped and looked toward Keith.

Mrs. Judbury nodded. "His poor wife lived on without friend or relative to look out for her wants. The same folks that had been all fired up about innocent people being called witches now began saying that the real witch hadn't been hung. What did they do was take to saying that Dame Judbury herself had cast a spell on her husband, driven him to hang himself, they said. As I heard it, they wouldn't have a thing to do with her, blaming her for every bit of bad luck that had happened since she came to live in the cove."

Once more Mrs. Judbury paused. A flash of lightning glared in the sky, and a clap of thunder sounded closer.

"Then, poor soul, one winter's day, so the story goes, somebody over in the village noticed there wasn't so much as a puff of smoke coming from the cottage chimney here. But it wasn't for another day that anyone thought to find out why."

Mrs. Judbury cleared her throat.

"What had happened?" Laurie asked softly.

"Dead she was," Mrs. Judbury said in a hard voice. "Poor soul, all alone, no neighborly help. Maybe sick. The long and short of it was that they found her down there frozen stiff. Frozen stiff," she repeated, "from the soles of her little silver-buckled shoes to the cap she wore on her poor head."

"How awful!" Shirley exclaimed. "You'd think the villagers would have hated the sight of that cottage after what happened there and knowing they'd been so cruel."

Mrs. Judbury shrugged. "Well, they did steer clear of it and began calling it Witch's Hollow. And the rise became known as Hangman's Hill—probably because of the hanging here. The Judbury brother claimed the place, and it stayed in the family until the Snows bought it."

"Well, I'd have torn down the cottage if I'd been Mrs. Snow," Laurie said. "Goodness, I'd be afraid of ghosts."

"She couldn't. When my husband finally inherited this property from his father, and sold it to the Snows, it was right in the contract that Witch's Hollow would not be torn down, used, nor repaired. It was my husband's idea that it should stand as a reminder to folks not to"—she hesitated, and swallowed hard—"not to be *mean*," she finished. "But I hate that cottage myself."

Keith frowned. "Then why don't you have it torn down?" he asked.

Mrs. Judbury stared in amazement. "*Me* have it

torn down!" she repeated. "But it was right in the legal paper it was to stand."

"But wasn't that agreement one the Snows had to keep?" Keith asked. "Why couldn't a Judbury tear it down?"

Mrs. Judbury's eyes shone. "Why not!" she exclaimed.

"Please," Shirley said nervously, "not while we're here. Maybe the Snows just love it, and we'd be sued or something if they came home from Europe and found, er—something missing."

But this did not seem to worry Mrs. Judbury. "I'll call the lawyer. Keith, you're a very bright young man! Now why on earth did I never think of that before?"

Keith grinned. "I can't imagine. I've *always* thought I was a bright young man."

Shirley laughed. "Well, I—"

She was interrupted by the sharp ring of the telephone. "I'll get it, Mom," Keith said.

"Keith, dear?" a horrible, squeaky, high-pitched voice crackled in Keith's ear. "There's a present for you and that darling family of yours. It's at your back door."

The line clicked dead.

Goosebumps lifted along Keith's arms. Slowly, he put down the phone. Then he called out toward the porch. "Wrong number, Mom. I'm going to get a glass of milk before I turn in."

"Good," Shirley called back. "Pour one for me, too. We'll all come out and have something."

"How dumb can I be," Keith thought. "All I

wanted to do was get to the kitchen by myself. Now, everybody will be there."

But there was one thing he was sure of—he didn't want the family to know whatever it was that waited outside in the dark.

THE NIGHT OF THE TOADS

☐ Mrs. Judbury put the cookie jar back on the shelf. "That thunder didn't come to anything after all," she said. "Not even a drop of rain."

"Thank goodness," Shirley yawned. "You know I believe I'll turn in."

"Turn in? It's awfully early," Laurie said.

Keith was on pins and needles. Any minute Pru might come back, and if she saw the "present" at the door, she'd be sure to bring it in.

"You look tired, too, Laurie," he urged. "You wouldn't have to sleep. You could go to bed and read."

Laurie's jaw dropped. "I could go to bed and read! Well, thanks for your permission, grandpa! But it so happens I have other plans!" she exploded.

"You are sounding sort of . . . of elderly, Keith," Shirley giggled, and pushed back her chair. "Well, work out your own lives, kids. Mom's saying good night."

When Keith heard his mother's footsteps on the stairs, he said, "Are you and Mrs. Judbury going to watch TV?"

Laurie stared at her brother. "Keith, what's wrong with you? Why don't you just come out and say it: 'will you kindly get out of the kitchen?' The answer is no. I'm waiting for Pru."

"So am I," Mrs. Judbury said.

"Okay," Keith said in a low voice. "But you may be sorry—and you've got to promise not to tell Mom."

Laurie and Mrs. Judbury exchanged puzzled glances. "What's up?" Laurie asked.

"When the phone rang, it wasn't a wrong number. Somebody said they'd left a 'present' at the kitchen door for our 'lovely family.' "

"Well, for goodness sake!" Laurie exclaimed. "Why shouldn't Mom know that? She's part of the family, isn't she?"

"Remember the greeting from The Hangman?" Keith asked. "Don't be stupid." He strode to the door.

"What hangman?" Mrs. Judbury demanded, trying to catch up with what was being said.

"Keith!" Laurie was after him in a flash. She caught at his belt. "Don't open the door. You can't tell what's out there."

"Let go of my belt," Keith demanded fiercely. "I said let go!"

Laurie released her hold so quickly that Keith nearly lost his balance. "Why don't you both go and sit down?" he asked coolly.

Meekly, Laurie and Mrs. Judbury walked back to the table, and Keith opened the door. Whatever the "present" might be, it wasn't gift-wrapped. A stained, string-tied, brown carton bearing a soiled white card rested at the kitchen entrance.

Quickly, Keith picked it up and went back into the kitchen.

"It may be a bomb!" Laurie quivered.

"Not unless witches are stewing up a new brew," Keith said dryly. "Look." He put the box on the table.

Scrawled across the card in thick black letters were the words, "A little present from—The Witch."

Mrs. Judbury's face turned pale. "I'll get a knife for cutting the string," she said in a hard, strange voice.

"Don't bother," Keith said as he gave the string a sharp tug and loosened it enough to be pulled off.

"Laurie," he warned, "if you think you're going to yell or something, just don't look. I don't want Mom coming downstairs. Okay?"

Laurie nodded and Keith pulled back the top flaps.

There was a tiny muffled shriek from Laurie as two dark, bumpy, brown shapes shot up in the air, then jumped, stunned, to the floor.

Toads. Toad catcher Pru's witch pets!

Mrs. Judbury, pale as death, bent down and picked up each little body. She quickly went toward the door. "I'll put these poor things down in the grass," she said. "They're not dead."

The door opened and Pru walked in.

"Hold the door, Prudence," Mrs. Judbury said. She stepped past her daughter and went outside.

"What's going on?" Pru asked, looking puzzled.

"As though you didn't know!" Keith said angrily. "Did you catch them fresh or were you saving them for tonight?"

Laurie looked as puzzled as Pru. "Keith, what on earth are you talking about? You don't think Pru sent those toads!"

"Yes, I think so!" Keith exclaimed. "And I think you have a great telephone voice, Pru." He picked up the carton. "Here—maybe you'll want to use this again. Catch!"

With those words, he tossed it toward Pru. As it tumbled through the air, a small crumpled tissue-wrapped package fell out, hit the floor, and skidded almost to Mrs. Judbury's feet as she stepped back into the kitchen.

A sudden quiet came over the group as she bent to pick it up.

Silently, she held the package in her hands. Her face went even paler. She shuddered.

"What is it, Mother? What's wrong?" Pru asked anxiously.

Mrs. Judbury didn't answer. She looked over at Keith and Laurie and said, "It's a hateful thing. Take it," she said, her voice trembling as she held out the package.

Keith walked over to her, and strangely, hot anger changed to deadly chill as his hand closed over the package.

As he tore off the wrappings, all thoughts of Pru went out of his head. There, lying in crumpled tissue, was a jeweled dog collar and two familiar metal tags, one lettered, SIMONE PARTRIDGE.

There was a moan from Laurie as she lurched over to a chair.

"Pru," Mrs. Judbury snapped, "fetch ice. Laurie's about to faint."

"No, I'm not," Laurie whispered. But she bent her head down on her arms. "Oh, Keith! Who could be so cruel?"

"That's what we mean to find out," Mrs. Judbury answered grimly. "And we'll begin now."

She looked at Keith. "Maybe you'd better start by

telling Pru and me about that 'hangman' you mentioned. Seems like someone is trying to make the Judburys look pretty bad."

Keith hesitated. His sense of fairness struggled with his suspicions. Then he made up his mind. If Pru was at the bottom of this, now was the time to find out.

"Okay, Mrs. Judbury," he said slowly. "But I have to have your word first—what we talk about doesn't get back to my mother. And you'll answer questions I have."

"Don't discuss it with him, Mother," Pru said angrily. "I think he ought to apologize."

Mrs. Judbury's face looked sad. She shook her head. "No, Prudence. Keith and Laurie are feeling pretty bad about their pet. If Keith thinks you had a part in his dog's disappearance and in this wicked act of sending the collar back in the black of night, then we want to know why. Now sit down and we'll have this out."

Keith took a deep breath. It was one thing to say what he thought to Pru, and another to tell a girl's mother why he thought what he did about her.

"It started Monday night," he said. "First thing, Simone disappears. Then Laurie and I come back from Haunt Port and see a dummy dangling from that 'hanging tree.' I've stowed it up in the closet along with the note on it that said, 'Welcome—The Hangman.'

"The next morning I see Pru down in the cove. She catches a toad. Most girls I know have sort of outgrown toad catching by the time they're Pru's age. But she seems to think it is some sort of great art. And then she says she wouldn't camp in the cove, but won't say why not.

"Then I go to Parsons' store for the groceries, and

I hear"—he flushed red but went on—"I hear Mr. Beresford call you and Pru 'the village witch and her weird witch daughter.'"

Pru angrily shoved back her chair, but her mother's bony hand closed down on her shoulder. "Go on," she ordered Keith.

"Then we hear from Mr. Beresford about how the kids shouldn't camp in the cove. But that's no more than Pru said.

"Now that's all on Tuesday. Wednesday morning we find our telephone line has been cut. Anybody with snippers could have done it when nobody was looking—and there was plenty of time between when Mother used the phone Tuesday afternoon and when she tried it that night after dinner. Pru was here all of that time.

"Then tonight I take a phone call and a high, squeaky voice says there's a present for my 'darling family' at the back door. Pru could have made that call from Haunt Port.

"And when I saw those toads—well, Pru *could* have put that box there. Plus all that, she's brought a cat here. I think she *knew* there wouldn't be a dog around. And last, you folks hate Haunt Port and wouldn't even show up for a . . . a public-spirited clambake. I think Pru hates everybody so much that it's just gotten to be a habit. Hating us would be her idea of fun, like toad catching."

There was a hush around the table. Then Keith spoke again. "Okay, I said I'd tell you and I did. Now you tell me where I'm wrong."

Laurie's voice trembled. "Before you do, I want to put it on the record—I don't believe you did any of this, Pru. I like you a lot."

Mrs. Judbury cleared her throat. "Well, now," she said. "Prudence, what have you to say for yourself?"

Pru sat straight as a stick. Dark eyes blazed as she pushed her black hair from her thin, tense face. "I never saw your dog in my life," she said, each word separate and hard. "And if there are two words I hate, they're 'hangman' and 'witch.' I don't own a pair of snippers and didn't cut your telephone line. And I didn't telephone you, either. And I wouldn't be so mean to toads as to put them in an airless box. But there's one thing you're right about, Keith Partridge —I hate Haunt Port and I hate most people. In fact, between you and a toad I'd pick a toad any day. At least a toad isn't mean."

She turned to Laurie. "I've liked you, too. But you don't have to stick up for me. I'm just sorry Mother's lost her job on my account."

Mrs. Judbury spoke for the first time. "Your mother hasn't lost her job and doesn't intend to."

"You mean you'll stay here after this?" Pru exclaimed.

"Of course, I will," Mrs. Judbury said. "Do you think I'm going to leave Mrs. Partridge in the lurch just because Keith has things figured wrong? Now, it's my turn to talk and I want you to listen as hard as I expect Keith will, Prudence."

She looked at Keith. "There are two main things you haven't much thought of as far as I can see. First, somebody's trying to scare you away from here—"

"That was the *first* thing I thought of," Keith said scornfully.

"For what reason? Did you decide on that?" Mrs. Judbury asked.

Keith shook his head.

"Well, it isn't likely the Judburys want you to leave. I work to earn money," Mrs. Judbury said crisply.

"Now second," she continued, "if you agree with that, you have to begin thinking of who would benefit if the house stood empty. The Parsons? No. Why would they want to lose a customer like your mother? Your neighbor, Mr. Beresford? About the worst you can say about that man is that he puts on airs. I can't imagine him skulking about cutting telephone lines and stealing dogs. If he talked mean about Pru and me, it's no more than Haunt Port folks have done.

"Next, and last, as all these happenings have been mean and not dangerous, I'd say—put it down to mean pranksters."

"Some pranksters!" Keith exclaimed. "I don't call what may have happened to Simone a prank. Poor Simone!"

As though in answer to her name, there was a weak woof at the door. Laurie sprang up from the table and in almost one bound flung it open.

There stood a much thinner, bedraggled, and trembling poodle.

"Simone!" Laurie cried. She gathered up the poodle in her arms. "Oh, Simone!"

After Simone had a bowl of milk with an egg whipped through it, she, and everybody, felt better.

Even Pru managed at least a calmer look around the table. "That dog will tell us where she's been," she said.

"How do you mean?" Keith asked, puzzled.

"You don't think she's going to wag her tail at the one who's been starving her, do you?" Pru asked.

"Gosh! You're right." Keith looked at Pru. "I'm sorry, Pru. Everything just seemed to fit."

"And now your other question was going to be, 'Why do people say you're a witch?' Wasn't it, Keith?" Mrs. Judbury asked. "And I'll tell you right now before I change my mind. Sometimes I know things before they happen. Years ago I was foolish enough to tell them. Mr. Judbury warned me against it, but I always thought I was helping by doing it.

"Then the time came when I had one of my bad feelings and I knew something had happened to Mr. Judbury out at sea. A fisherman he was then with the little Haunt Port fleet. I made Dr. Simms come to the wharf to meet the boats.

"Indeed, something had happened, but it was too late to help. Mr. Judbury was taken bad when they pulled in the nets. Dr. Simms being there didn't matter."

At that point Pru broke in angrily. "And so they said it was pretty strange, Mother knowing and all. They almost called her a . . . a poisoner, but they settled later for witch."

Laurie's eyes filled with tears of sympathy, but Keith pushed back his chair, glaring at Pru. "So ever since you've done your best, I guess, to show them they were right—that you were the witch's daughter! I don't suppose it ever entered your head to prove them wrong by trying to make people *like* you. It was easier to be nice to toads!"

"Keith!" Laurie exclaimed.

"No. I mean it. Don't you *read* in that school you

go to? Haven't you ever heard of ESP or precognition or psychometry?" Keith asked. "Why would knowing about the future make your mother a witch? You've just gone along with the townspeople."

"Psychometry?" Mrs. Judbury asked. "What's that?"

"Well, like holding something in your hand and . . . and getting a feeling about it," Keith said. "As you did with Simone's collar. And precognition is knowing about what's going to happen. Gosh! Mrs. Judbury, maybe you'd be famous at a place like . . . like Duke University, where they study things like that!"

Mrs. Judbury, half smiling, stood up. "Right now I get a strange feeling that breakfast is the next thing I see in the future. Let's say good night."

As she stalked off, Laurie flung her arms around Pru, Pru returned the hug and Keith muttered something about, "Let's make things different around here."

It wasn't until Mrs. Judbury reached her bedroom door that it happened.

Just as she put her hand on the doorknob, a dark, calm sea seemed to flood before her eyes and take the place of the familiar hallway. And the clapping sound of wading seemed to sound in her ears. Dark, dark! And then came a vision of the white beam of light.

Mrs. Judbury raised her hands across her eyes as though to shut out the glare. What did it mean? Quietly, she turned the knob, then closed the bedroom door behind her.

DANNY'S DISCOVERY

☐ It was a beautiful, cool August morning. After breakfast the Partridges didn't lose a beat in beginning the first rehearsal of their vacation.

Soon the air was filled with their music—music they shaped themselves into their very own style. Rock, swing, bend, soar—it sounded out on the morning air.

And it was Shirley, not the kids, who finally called it quits at almost eleven o'clock. "How about a before-lunch swim?" she asked.

"Let's run through that one more time, Mom," Keith suggested.

"Well, okay!" Shirley grinned, tapped her foot. "Ah-one . . ."

Before she could beat out "ah-two," the telephone rang. It was Jane Parsons calling Laurie.

Her voice crackled over the wire.

"Laurie? This is an awful connection. Can you hear me?"

"Sure."

"Listen, Laurie, I have a problem. Last night my

cousin, Bailey Parsons, called us from the airport in Boston. He's on his way home to California from Europe. Anyhow, he said he'd promised his mother and father to call us. And Laurie," Jane groaned, "Dad insisted on Bailey's stopping off here to visit us for a few days. Dad's gone into Boston to bring him back and another boy—the one Bailey's in Europe with."

Laurie laughed. "That doesn't sound like such a problem. Are they in college someplace?"

"Not unless Bailey is a genius," Jane answered. "He's about my age. I've been hearing about him all my life. And that's the problem—I've never seen him. He may be perfectly awful, and his friend, too."

"I know how you feel," Laurie replied sympathetically. "But he may be okay and maybe he won't stay too long."

"But wait. I haven't told you everything," Jane said. "Mother wants you and Keith to come to our place and bring Pru—if you can imagine! You see, she's Bailey's cousin, too. It's sort of complicated. Anyhow, Mother's going to call up herself."

"Why couldn't you people come here instead?" Laurie asked. "I mean, everything's planned. We were going to have a cook-out in the cove. Actually, it would be a lot more fun—you know, with more people."

Jane sighed. "Well, I'll tell Mother, but I don't know. I guess she feels she should entertain Bailey; you know, so he'll tell his family what lovely relatives they have in the East."

Laurie giggled. "Cheer up. We can live through it if you can. Now what's next? We wait for your mother's call, or what?"

"Wait," Jane answered. "I'll speak to Mother in the meantime."

As Laurie hung up the phone, Pru came in from the kitchen. "You sounded wonderful rehearsing, Laurie," she said. "Wish I could sing!"

Laurie took a deep breath. "Pru, Jane Parsons just called. She said her mother is calling your mother. It's about tonight."

Briefly, she told Pru about Bailey Parsons and Mrs. Parsons' invitation. "So which would you rather, Pru —go there or have them come here? It may go either way, but don't say 'neither' because you're absolutely *stuck!*"

It finally was decided that Chief Parsons would drop off Jane and the visitors at seven o'clock.

After one more run-through of their latest number, the family went into Haunt Port, and a motorboat was rented for the rest of their stay. It had to be tried out, and the kids spent the afternoon swimming and whizzing around the cove with Captain Keith. Before anybody wanted to stop, it was time to pull the boat ashore and go up to the beach house.

"What is this, anyhow?" Chris demanded. "Mom, you're going to a party at Mr. Beresford's, and Keith and Laurie are having a party without us."

Shirley laughed. "Keith and Laurie don't go to all of the parties you go to, do they? Besides, I'll bet you couldn't wait until eight o'clock to eat!"

"Eight o'clock!" Danny gasped. "Man! I can't wait until six o'clock."

Chris scowled. "I don't trust anybody over fifteen these days." Then he grinned. "Okay, me and Danny

and Tracy will let them have their old party." Then
he added warningly, "But we're going to have more
fun, I bet."

Much to Jane's relief, her unknown Cousin Bailey
turned out to be about all any cousin could hope for.
And his friend, Bill Angelo, was as Laurie said, "terribly attractive."

"Your mother certainly turns out a great blueberry
pie, Pru," Bill grinned.

Jane laughed. "I'll bet Pru's mother and mine probably took blueberry pie lessons from the same aunt.
Which one do you think it was, Pru?"

"Probably somebody with a name like Zenobia
Quackenberry," Bailey chuckled. "Man! Our family
names really get me."

"Hey! Look at the moon!" Laurie exclaimed. "It's
coming up like a yellow balloon!"

Bailey and Bill said that they'd never seen such a
sight over the Pacific.

"But you must have beautiful sunsets," Pru said
shyly, the only sentence she had uttered since the
guests had arrived.

"Sure do. You come out there, Pru, and I'll show
you the greatest sunsets you've ever seen," Bill answered.

Pru smiled. "I'd like to. Maybe I'll see the world
one of these days."

"Kee-ith! Laur-ree!" Mrs. Judbury shouted from
the top of the rock path. "Are the children there with
you?"

Keith looked up. "No. They haven't been here at
all."

"Well, then, you'd better come up and help me find them. They've disappeared."

Laurie and Pru scrambled to their feet. "But there's no place for them to *go*," Laurie said, puzzled.

"No? Only the whole Atlantic Ocean," Keith exclaimed, springing up.

"You don't suppose they decided to drop in at Mr. Beresford's party, do you?" Laurie asked, ignoring Keith's awful suggestion.

"Who knows?" Keith answered. "But come on. Let's start looking."

"We'll help," the three visitors said.

Keith and Laurie sprinted far in the lead. "They must be hiding on purpose," Laurie said crossly. "Probably they were mad because they weren't invited to eat with us."

Keith shook his head. "They've never pulled anything like that." He started to stride into the house and then stopped. "I don't know why I'm going in here. There's no place for them to hide."

"Well, they're not down on the ocean side. I looked there first thing," Mrs. Judbury said.

"Then where can they be?" Laurie asked, no longer cross but really worried.

"I can't think," Mrs. Judbury answered. "I was watching television and Danny came to the porch and said, 'Come here, Chris. I want to show you something.' So Chris got up and Tracy tagged along. Then first thing I knew, they just weren't anywhere."

Keith thought a minute. "They must be in the house. They're probably hiding on purpose and giggling their heads off."

The other volunteers came walking up. "Maybe

they're hiding in a closet," Pru said. "Laurie, let's look upstairs."

"Wait until I get my hands on them," Laurie muttered. "Okay. Let's look. You want to come, too, Jane?"

"We'll take the downstairs," Keith said, striding off with Bailey and Bill behind him.

It took no more than three minutes for a searching posse of six people to look into every closet in the beach house. There was no sign of the missing children.

"Maybe we should call Mother," Laurie said uncertainly.

"That's dumb. What could she do?" Keith answered.

Laurie was near tears. "But what can *we* do? That's the point!"

"Maybe I should call Dad," Jane suggested. "I mean, if they'd taken a notion to go for a walk along the road, or something—"

Pru suddenly lifted her hand. "Ssh! Do you hear that? Listen!"

There was a dull faraway-sounding thump. "I heard it," Laurie whispered.

"Where's it coming from?" Bailey asked. "I heard it, too."

There was another thump and another and another. And now the direction was clear. The noises were coming from right in the middle of the big beach house.

Keith rushed to the living-room wall and batted his hand against the wood paneling. An answering thump came immediately.

"Maybe there's a secret panel!" Laurie cried.

Everybody went to the paneling and, movie style, began pressing around for a hidden spring. Nothing happened.

"Let's try the wall on the other side," Pru suggested. All but Mrs. Judbury went racing into the kitchen and on into the long hallway that ran parallel to the living room. No luck. Thumps answered thumps, but no secret panel swung back.

"The closet!" Pru cried. "The one between the kitchen and the hallway." She ran back, opened the door, and reaching in beyond the brooms, mops, and pail, pressed the back wall.

It swung backward. "Danny?" she called sharply.

A wail greeted her. Tracy. Nobody could wail quite like Tracy Partridge.

The searchers in the hallway came crowding to the closet door.

"Danny Partridge!" Keith called into the dark. "You come out from there."

"Come on, Tracy," Laurie called over Keith's shoulder. "Where's that flashlight, Keith?"

Footsteps sounded high above them. "It's a staircase!" Laurie said in amazement. "A secret staircase!"

A grimy, perspiry, red-faced Chris was first to emerge, with Tracy close behind, weeping and hanging onto the back of her brother's jersey. Last came Danny, equally damp and red-faced but managing to look as though he had been doing something very clever.

"Now what is this?" Keith asked sternly.

"You don't need to sound mad," Danny said. "I

should think you would be glad to see us. We might have suffocated."

"That's why I'm mad," Keith answered. "What were you doing?"

"Well, I began thinking about the secret staircase in the House of the Seven Gables," Danny answered. "So I started measuring this place. And I figured the living-room wall and the hall were three feet apart. So I began looking around, and I looked in the broom closet and then I sort of stumbled over the cleaning pail and—gosh!—the wall opened!"

"So you called your brother and sister and didn't tell Mrs. Judbury, and got stuck. Some explorer you are! You might have been there forever. We could hardly hear you."

"The door just shut behind us," Chris said. "Just like in the movies. Don't you even want to know what we found?"

"What?"

"Stairsteps," Chris answered.

"Where did they go?"

"Up," said Danny. "I was thinking—maybe I would write a book. I'd call it The Case of the Missing Staircase. I bet a book like that could pay our entire vacation expenses."

"Right now I'd say that three expensive baths are needed," Mrs. Judbury said. "This looks like a three-bar soap emergency to me."

After the members of Expedition Staircase had gone to the second floor with Mrs. Judbury, Bailey Parsons began chuckling. "That's a pretty smart kid."

"Too smart for our own good," Keith replied. "He sure ended our beach party."

"We could go back," Laurie said. "In fact, we'd better. All those paper plates and stuff are lying around."

"I'll get the flashlight," Keith said.

"And your guitar?" Jane asked. "Would you play for us?"

"Sure," Keith smiled, "if anybody will sing."

When Mr. Beresford swung up the beach house drive, the soft glow of a campfire showed above the rocks.

"Listen!" Shirley exclaimed. "Hear that singing? The kids are having a good time."

Mr. Beresford said, "I'm afraid it's not my kind of music."

Shirley nodded. "Your tastes are very different. Your record collection shows that. I loved your paintings. And I loved every bit of the evening. It was so kind of you to include me in your party."

Mr. Beresford smiled. "So nice of you to come. I wish I could look forward to inviting you and Mr. Kinkaid this weekend, but alas! I must be in the city. Perhaps the following weekend?"

Shirley shook her head. "No. We'll be ending our vacation next week."

"When?" Mr. Beresford asked sharply.

"Oh, not until the very last minute. We're having such a good time!"

They said good night, and Mr. Beresford headed his car back along the drive.

KEITH CAN'T SLEEP

☐ The next morning rehearsal went off without a hitch. In fact, it was one of the best they'd had. Shirley took a deep breath of the sparkling air that smelled of sun and sea. "The kids needed this," she thought. "In spite of storms and secret staircases, it's been good for them to get away."

Nevertheless, there *was* something spooky about a secret staircase.

"Why do you suppose the Snows ever built that staircase?" she asked as she helped Mrs. Judbury with the lunch sandwiches.

Mrs. Judbury shrugged. "No more than a notion is my guess. By the look of those three children last night, that staircase hasn't seen any use since the day it was built. I'd count on that."

Shirley nodded and looked at her watch. "I wonder where everybody scattered? Just this wonderful sea air would tell *me* it's lunchtime!"

"I've a notion Pru and Laurie are showing off the sailboat to Bailey Parsons and that nice Bill Angelo. And probably Keith is taking Jane Parsons for a spin around the cove. It looks to me, Mrs. Partridge, as though we'll have six happy kids at the clambake tomorrow night."

"And I think you're right," Shirley answered. "Here come three of them now."

Mrs. Judbury looked up. "I don't see Pru," she said worriedly. "I wonder what's happened?"

She soon found out. "Bill Angelo is taking over my sailing lesson time with Pru," Laurie giggled. "And anyone with half an eye could see he already knows all about boats."

And Keith grinned. "We were all invited by Mrs. Parsons to have lunch aboard the *Lavinia Jane*, but we said we had to come back to rehearse. So Mrs. Parsons said, 'Well, Pru doesn't have to rehearse, does she?' And to make a long story short, Pru won't be here for lunch."

Mrs. Judbury tried hard not to look too pleased. "It will make little difference in making sandwiches," she said. "And that's what I have my mind on."

Shirley and the kids almost winked at each other. Things certainly were taking a change for the better in the Judbury family.

"And I have my mind on lunch, and on rehearsal after that," Shirley said. "Keith, will you call the kids? They're living off the land again, down in the cove."

As Keith reached the top of the path, he could see that whatever the kids were doing it wasn't living off the land. All three were kneeling at the boarded-up entrance of the old cottage.

"Hey, kids! Lunch!"

There was something about the quick way his younger brothers and sister bobbed up that gave Keith the feeling he should go down the path and see what was going on.

"Here we come," Tracy called sweetly. "You needn't come down."

Keith hesitated. After the success of Expedition Staircase, maybe Danny had decided to investigate everything in sight.

"You weren't trying to get into the cottage, were you?" he asked, as Danny trailed the others up the path.

"Oh," Danny replied, "I don't think we could."

Keith sighed. "That isn't the point. It's boarded up —to keep people *out*."

They had almost reached the beach house when Chris, who had gone on ahead, came racing back from the doorway to meet them. "Say, Danny! What'd you think? We don't have to rehearse at all! Mr. Beresford's taking you and me and Tracy and Mom out on his big boat this afternoon!"

"Man!" Danny exclaimed. "Will that be great!" Then his face changed. "But how come he didn't ask Keith and Laurie? Can't they come, too?"

Keith, who had felt like bopping Danny Partridge only a second before, suddenly felt that being a member of the Partridge Family was about the best thing that could ever have happened to anybody.

"'One for all and all for one'—that's us," he thought. But he answered gruffly, "Mr. Beresford doesn't happen to have an ocean-going liner, Danny. A boat's a boat, you know. There's not room for everybody."

"Besides, they're invited next week," Chris explained.

Keith Partridge was sure of one thing—he wouldn't go around the block with Mr. Beresford, let alone around the Atlantic. "If everybody else likes him, okay," he thought. "But there's something wrong with that guy." He shook his head. "If I could only think of what it was he said that morning in the cove! He said *something* that didn't match up."

It hadn't been hard to persuade Shirley that an afternoon's cruise would be fun. She and the younger children started off with Mr. Beresford, and the others joined Jane Parsons and her guests. Mrs. Judbury had the afternoon to herself.

Calling to Benjamina, she went striding off for a close look at the Witch's Hollow cottage.

"I don't know why on earth I have that cottage on my mind today," she said to herself as she made her way over the rocks.

It suddenly struck Mrs. Judbury that except for the tilting line of the roof, the cottage looked remarkably sturdy. "It was built tight and strong, of course," she thought. "Still, it's had over three hundred years of Atlantic gales blowing around it, and yet there's not a shingle loose or curling. It doesn't seem reasonable." She sat down by the boarded-up door and leaned back, and Benjamina settled herself down in the shade.

Immediately, something point-sharp pressed against her shoulder, and for a moment Mrs. Judbury shivered. It was as though the hated cottage was hating back. Then carefully she leaned forward and as carefully ran her fingers over her shoulder. Nothing was there. She stood up, turned, and examined the boarding. No wonder she had felt something sharp! A long splinter of wood stood out at an angle. She snapped it off.

"Now that's funny!" she thought. "This is green wood. But this place has been boarded up for years. Now how could that be? The boarding would be *old*."

There was only one answer—it was new boarding. And someone had taken the trouble to stain it to make it look old and weathered.

Mrs. Judbury closely examined the nail heads driven into the boarding. Then she squinted along the edge of the outer boards. "Wish I'd brought my spectacles," she thought. "There's something funny about this. Oh, well, what I can't see I can touch—but I'll still have to go up and get a knife."

She hurried back to the beach house and returned with a firm-bladed table knife and her spectacles.

Working quickly, she slid the knife between the boarding and the cottage wall. Not one driven nail stopped the swift upward stroke of the knife. The nailed-tight boarding wasn't nailed tight at all. *It was a complete fake!*

"Hi, Mrs. Judbury!" Keith called down from the top of the path.

Just as Chris, Danny, and Tracy had sprung away from the door, now Mrs. Judbury whirled to face Keith. For the second time that day Keith wondered what was so interesting about that door.

But now was not the time to find out. Jane and

Laurie, followed by Bill and Bailey, came trooping to the top of the rocks. They were all in swim-gear and carrying towels and beach blankets.

Mrs. Judbury forgot about the door in her pleasure at seeing Pru laughing with the others. She also forgot the table knife in her hand, brandishing it in a silvery, flashing greeting.

"I see we left a knife down here last night," Laurie said. "Gosh! I thought we'd picked up everything."

Mrs. Judbury blushed. "Well, no harm done," she said lamely. "I suppose I have a bunch of customers for snacks later?"

"Oh, don't bother with us," Keith answered. "We'll pick up something."

"That's what I was asking," Mrs. Judbury replied. "I'll go fix something for you to pick up."

It had been a wonderful day, and Keith Pattridge should have been as sound asleep as anybody under the beach house roof. But at 3:30 in the morning, he was wide awake listening to the swish and thud of the ocean waves on the rocks below. Not only was he wide awake—he was worried.

Right in the middle of thinking that Jane Parsons would be the girl he would most like to spend a clambake with, Mr. Beresford had come leaping into his mind.

In no explainable way, Keith suddenly had his answer to what had been dimly bothering him ever since that morning Mr. Beresford came down to Witch's Hollow.

"Mother said our dog was lost. Then he said,

'Maybe someone picked it up. Poodles are valuable.'
How did Mr. Beresford know Simone was a poodle?
Nobody said so."

Keith sat bolt upright in bed. "*Because he stole Simone.* And *he* sent those toads and her collar. But why?"

He flung back the covers and reached for his bathrobe. Suddenly, he felt the need for something everyday and normal, like electric lights and a glass of milk. Silently he padded along the hallway and down the stairs.

When he reached the kitchen doorway, his heart made a tremendous thump. A gigantically tall, shadowy figure outlined in moonlight sat motionless at the kitchen table.

For a second Keith nearly turned and ran. Then common sense and the sight of Benjamina's dark silhouette came to his rescue, and he realized Mrs. Judbury was the figure at the table.

"Is that you, Keith?" She spoke in a quiet voice.

"Yes. I came down for a glass of milk."

"I was waiting for you."

Keith nearly bolted out of the kitchen.

THE SECRET OF WITCH'S HOLLOW

☐ It took all of Keith's will power to hang onto the idea that the dark witchlike figure seated at the kitchen table was only Mrs. Judbury by moonlight.

"Do you mind if I turn on the lights?" he managed to say.

"Go ahead."

The second the light was on, Keith wondered how he could have had goosebumps only a moment before.

Mrs. Judbury, bundled in a blurry brown and yellow flannel bathrobe, her iron-gray hair hanging in a pigtail, looked more like a hard-working pioneer woman than a sinister witch. And certainly, there was nothing chilling in her next words. "The cookies are in the first cupboard on the second shelf."

"Thanks."

"If you'd put on the kettle, I'd have a cup of tea while you're drinking your milk."

By 3:30 A.M. conversation was going along naturally, even though the topic was unusual. "Mrs. Judbury," Keith said slowly, "why did you say you were 'waiting' for me? Did you really know I was going to come downstairs?"

Mrs. Judbury nodded.

"Did you know why I'd come down?" Keith asked.

Mrs. Judbury hesitated. "It had something to do with Witch's Hollow, didn't it?"

Keith started to shake his head. Then suddenly the scene down in the cove seemed to float before his eyes —Mr. Beresford warning them about camping down there, and all the talk about witches.

He stared at Mrs. Judbury in amazement. "I guess you're right," he said. "But it wasn't really Witch's Hollow, it was Mr. Beresford—something he said there."

Mrs. Judbury listened carefully as Keith told her of the slip Mr. Beresford had made. "The funny thing is, I couldn't think of it at all. Then all of a sudden it just popped into my head as though I hadn't forgotten it at all."

Mrs. Judbury nodded. "And I'll bet you that you thought of it when you weren't trying to think of it. That's usually the way those things happen, I've found." She sighed. "That's why I'm having such a hard time getting the answer to what's bothering me. I'm thinking too hard about it."

She sipped her tea. "You know, when all of you were away this afternoon, I went down to Witch's Hollow. I told myself I ought to look at it. But why look at an old, empty, boarded-up, miserable cottage?"

Keith waited for her to go on.

"Now why? Same reason you had for thinking about Mr. Beresford. You thought there was something not right about Mr. Beresford. I think there is something not right about Witch's Hollow. And I also think somebody doesn't want the Partridges around here. And somebody doesn't want the Judburys around here, either."

Keith's eyes widened. "Judburys? It seems to me that everything's been happening to the Partridges."

"Well, if you were scared off, Pru and I wouldn't be here either, would we?"

Keith sighed. "Well, you're right. But *why?* I just don't get it. Look," he motioned to the window. "It's getting light." The sky was no longer black, but a thick, cold gray.

Mrs. Judbury shivered. "I've never been one to be crazy about the dawn," she said. "To me, it's always seemed the deadly time."

She put down her stone-cold teacup. "There's one thing I haven't told you," she said slowly. "And I don't know as I should."

"My gosh, Mrs. Judbury. That's an awful thing to say. How could I go back to bed now?"

Mrs. Judbury was silent for a moment. "Well, I'll have to have your word to keep a secret and trust me."

Keith laughed. "This is over my head, but okay—I trust you."

Quickly she told him of her discovery of the fake boarding on the cottage door.

"Well, why didn't you say so right off!" Keith exclaimed. "Here we've been talking about everything else, and probably the whole explanation is right under our noses."

Then a thought struck him. "Chris and the kids

must be onto it, too," he said. "They were certainly interested in that doorway this morning."

"Then there's no time to lose!" Mrs. Judbury exclaimed. She jumped up. "Where's the flashlight, Keith?"

Keith's ESP told him that Mrs. Judbury was about to go down to Witch's Hollow without him. "I'll put on my sneakers first," he said. "I'll be right back."

And completely forgetting his lecture to Chris on not prying into boarded-up places, he rushed off.

Following Mrs. Judbury's six-feet-three outline in the silent, chilly, gray dawn, Keith had a feeling that he was trapped in a strange dream. Wet grass slapped at his ankles, and damp cold went straight through the sweater he had hastily exchanged for his robe. He carried a table knife in one hand and a pair of pliers, in case they were needed, in the other. Mrs. Judbury had commandeered the flashlight.

Not until they'd made their stumbling way over the rocks and reached the cottage did Mrs. Judbury switch on the light. Even then, she was careful to stand between its beam and Haunt Port. "No need for any early bird to wonder what's going on over here," she said.

As she had suspected, concealed hinges fastened the boarding on one side, but the other side and the top were free of nail fastenings. She bent down in the wet weeds. "I guarantee there's a spring latch, or something, at the bottom of this."

She ran her fingers beneath the boarding edge. "Here's something," and pressed against it. Nothing happened.

"Here. Let me try," Keith said.

Mrs. Judbury rose and stood back. Keith got down on his freezing knees and felt the metal beneath the door edge. "Chris must have seen something from the outside," he said. "Let's shine the flash down here."

It was a good try. A round piece of metal, no bigger than a nail head, projected about a quarter-inch from the board surface. Keith pressed it and heard a small "click."

"Try the side now," he told Mrs. Judbury.

Mrs. Judbury slipped the table knife into the narrow slot between the boarding and the wall. She pressed it toward her. Keith scrambled out of the way as the boarding became a complete door that swung silently back on its well-oiled hinges.

"Here goes!" Mrs. Judbury said, and started to step inside the old cottage.

Keith, remembering how Chris and the kids had been trapped, called out, "Wait!"

He found a stick on the ground and hastily propped back the door.

Then, Mrs. Judbury in the lead, they both stepped inside. Mrs. Judbury shone the flashlight ahead.

"Great Heavens!" she whispered in a hoarse, hushed voice.

"Man!" Keith breathed.

Directly before them in the eerie circle cast by the flashlight was a rough, huge tabletop. On it stood big jeweled goblets, shining, curved, steel scimitars and wicked-looking knives, all with heavily jeweled hilts. There were little boxes—shining gold and crusted with gleaming jewels. And ivory boxes, carved like lace. And over at one side were small carved figures in jade and ivory.

Mrs. Judbury circled the light around. On the floor were small wooden crates. On their tops were long tubes encased in water-proof wrappings. And propped up on the ancient fireplace mantel was a beautifully framed, very small oil painting, still nesting in its packing straw. Packing boards and straw littered the room.

Keith was too awestruck to move, but Mrs. Judbury cautiously stepped forward across the sagging old floor. She went to the fireplace and lifted the painting off the mantel. "This damp cottage is no place for a nice oil painting," she said in a practical voice. Carefully, she tucked it under her arm, then turned and said, "Let's go."

"Let's go!" Keith repeated in amazement. "Let's *look!*"

But Mrs. Judbury almost swept him out the door, dunking the flashlight as they stepped outside.

"What do we do now?" Keith whispered.

"Get back to the house before anybody sees me gallivanting around in my bathrobe," Mrs. Judbury whispered back. "I'll call Chief Parsons first thing after breakfast—soon as he's had time to wake up."

"No! Don't do that—of all things don't do that!" Keith exclaimed, grabbing at her arm.

"It's the only thing to do," Mrs. Judbury hissed. "This is stolen property."

Keith hung onto her flannel sleeve. "No! Call Chief Parsons and what happens? He'll call the county police and they'll call the government agents, probably.

And then what? They'll get the stuff. But we want to get whoever put it there, don't we?"

Mrs. Judbury hesitated. Then she shook her arm free and started up the rock path. Keith followed angrily but silently. "Who does she think I am?" he thought, growing angrier with every step. "Benjamina?"

"Mrs. Judbury, please trust me," he said in a low voice.

Mrs. Judbury stopped at the top of the path and turned to him.

"What about?"

"Just promise that you'll wait to call Chief Parsons until we talk about this. I have an idea. And if I'm right this is your big chance!"

Mrs. Judbury stared. "I can't imagine what you're talking about, but—well, can you get along with only a few hours' sleep?"

"Sleep! I couldn't sleep now!"

"Try. I'll call you at ten o'clock. Until then I promise—I won't do a thing until you've told me what's on your mind."

And as the east sky over the Atlantic rosied into a bright pink, Keith and Mrs. Judbury said good night.

MRS. JUDBURY'S ESP

☐ Sharp at ten o'clock, Mrs. Judbury knocked on Keith's door and called out loudly.

There was a muffled answer.

She thumped on the door again. "Are you really awake, or do I have to come in there and shake you?"

Sleepy as he was, the thought of Mrs. Judbury marching into his room was enough to rouse Keith. He swung his legs to the floor. "Okay," he called back. "I'm up. Thanks."

"Where's everybody?" he asked, when he came into the kitchen ten minutes later.

"Your mother and the children are half-way to Boston by now," Mrs. Judbury replied. "She wanted to do some shopping and get haircuts for the boys before Mr. Kinkaid's plane is due. They'll be back around four," she said. "And the girls are out on the cove, sailing.

"Now, Keith, I've kept my promise. What is this big chance of mine you're going to tell me about?"

Keith grinned. "Don't I get breakfast first?"

Mrs. Judbury handed him a glass of juice. "Start on this. I'll scramble the eggs."

As Keith finished his last piece of toast, Mrs. Judbury pulled back a chair and sat down at the table.

"You might as well know, I'm on pins and needles," she said, "and will be until that stolen property is in the right hands. So speak your piece. I'm waiting."

"Will you really *think* about my idea before you answer?" Keith asked.

"I'll let you have your say before I answer, if that's what you mean," Mrs. Judbury replied.

"Okay." He took a deep breath. "I want to move that stuff up here and stack it along the secret staircase."

Mrs. Judbury gasped. "Move it up *here!* For goodness sakes, why? So *we* can be arrested for stealing?"

Keith shook his head. "Ever since you told us you sometimes knew about things before they happened, I've been thinking—it would be pretty good if you could get started on a new kind of reputation. I mean, instead of people calling you a witch, they'd begin calling you 'that famous Mrs. Judbury who is a genuine psychic.'"

"Well, I *never!*" Mrs. Judbury exclaimed. "This is no time to be thinking about my reputation, I must say. And right now, about the only thing I know that is going to happen is that I'm going to call Thaddeus Parsons—and the sooner, the better." She started to rise.

"Wait!" Keith exclaimed. "You promised to listen."

Mrs. Judbury slowly sat down.

"What I was going to say is, we could move the stuff up here first, and *then* call Chief Parsons. He'd have to call the FBI or somebody, and then they could move in when you gave the signal."

"When I gave the *what?*"

"Well, why couldn't you, Mrs. Judbury? Why couldn't you put your ESP or precognition or whatever it is to work for your—er, country? Besides, the Chief is running for sheriff this fall. Think what it would mean to his reputation when people found out he's used the latest psychic methods in crime detection to capture maybe a big international gang of art thieves!"

Mrs. Judbury snorted. "I can just see Thaddeus Parsons agreeing to a hare-brained scheme like that! Who's to say I'd 'get the signal'? And if I did, what good would it do to catch thives down in the cove if the loot was up here? All they could be arrested for would be breaking and entering."

"Which is just what we've done," Keith answered.

"That was different," Mrs. Judbury replied indignantly. "I figure that cottage is as much mine as anybody's. And the picture I took—I brought it up here just to keep it safe."

"My gosh! That's what I'm *talking* about. Let's move *all* the stuff here to keep it safe. We can't watch that cottage all the time. But we'll be here for another week, and I'll bet something will happen before we go. That's why somebody's tried to scare us off. Somebody is going to come driving up and try to get that stuff they *think* is in the cottage."

A strange expression came into Mrs. Judbury's eyes, and Keith's words circled uneasily in her head. *Driving up.* No! Once more her vision of darkness, water, and the sound of sloshing wading came back to her. Whoever was coming was coming to *bring* more "stuff," and was coming by water.

"Mrs. Judbury, *please*," Keith begged. "You don't want to be a witch all your life, do you? Think of Pru!"

Mrs. Judbury scarcely heard him. "Keith, call Parsons' store," she ordered.

"You call," Keith replied bitterly. "It's your idea."

Mrs. Judbury paid no attention to his words. "Ask Lavinia Parsons for Mrs. Snow's address. She's bound to ask if something is wrong, so just say you want to write a letter, or something."

Keith stared. "Well, I can't imagine why, but okay."

Mrs. Judbury put on her spectacles and read the address Keith handed to her. "Hmm. London, England. That's just fine. We won't have language troubles with foreign telephone operators."

"Telephone operators?"

"Of course," Mrs. Judbury said calmly. "I mean to call Mrs. Snow and ask straight out for permission to tear down the cottage. If she says yes, we'd *have* to move everything, wouldn't we?"

Keith's eyes glowed. He made a dash for the phone. "Here's hoping she's not out someplace," he called back.

Mrs. Snow *was* in, and Keith listened to one of the shortest trans-Atlantic calls on record.

"Mrs. Snow? Increase Judbury in Haunt Port. I want to tear down the cove cottage. Is that all right with you? . . . No, the renters don't mind. . . . Well, fine. I'll say goodby. Goodby."

Mrs. Judbury put down the phone. "Well, I'm glad

to say that Mrs. Snow is not in cahoots with a gang of art thieves. She said yes, right off. Come on, Keith. Let's get started! I wish those girls would get back from sailing. We could use help."

By two o'clock that afternoon, with Pru, Laurie, Mrs. Judbury, and Keith hard at work, the staircase was packed nearly to the bottom step.

It was a glittering array of gold, silver, brass, twinkling jewels and, on the lower steps, were the crated narrow boxes which Mrs. Judbury was sure contained valuable oil paintings.

"That's that!" she exclaimed, wiping her perspiring forehead. "The way I feel now, I'm in no shape for a clambake!"

Pru, Laurie, and Keith exchanged quick surprised glances. Until that moment, they had no idea Mrs. Judbury was about to take part in the social life of Haunt Port. But something had evidently happened to change her mind.

"You'll feel better after a shower, Mother," Pru said. "And there will be plenty of time to rest before Mrs. Partridge and the children get back with Mr. Kinkaid."

Mrs. Judbury turned to Keith. "There's one last thing to be done." She reached into her apron pocket and took out a wad of packing material. "Keith, see how this matches up with that dummy you told me about. I don't know just what proof we'd have if it did, but check it out."

It was only a few minutes before Keith came galloping back to the kitchen. "We've got our man," he said excitedly. "This stuff matches up—burlap and stuffings! And man! Would I like to get the guy who did it!"

"We'll leave those details to the law," Mrs. Judbury replied. "Now why don't you all clean up and take a rest?"

"I feel like a swim," Laurie said.

Mrs. Judbury sighed. "Land alive! And here I was, feeling sorry for you!"

At the clambake that evening Reuben Kinkaid leaned back in a beach chair and watched the scene around him as people moved about, talking to friends, laughing, enjoying themselves.

"This is a great place!" he said to Mrs. Judbury. "What a wonderful town to grow up in. Look at those nice people! Not a mean thought in their heads. You can tell! These people are *real*, Mrs. Judbury."

Mrs. Judbury nodded. "They're real all right," she said. "I'll say that much."

She watched Prudence in the distance brushing butter on an ear of corn and handing it to Bill Angelo. "Thank goodness for the Partridges," she said under her breath. "Things aren't ever going to be the same around here. I'll swear to that!"

"Look at Keith," Mr. Kinkaid said. "Now there's a boy with not a care in the world."

Mrs. Judbury suddenly coughed. Then she said, "It looks as though the Partridge Family is going to give us a tune."

Reuben Kinkaid nodded. "I told them to go ahead. They're going to do the same program they'll be doing on Labor Day. We'll get a crowd reaction, and the folks here will have some fun."

The Partridge Family really rocked Haunt Port. Even the oldest graybeards were creakingly nodding their heads in time to the rock beat.

Only Mrs. Judbury was still and apart from all around her.

Something kept pulling her away—far away. And in that far distance, a ship seemed to glide in thick mist. And Mrs. Judbury could plainly see the black letters on its gray-painted sides—the *Turkish Rose.*

Unnoticed by Reuben Kinkaid, she quietly got up and made her way through the crowd to Chief Parsons.

"Thaddeus," she said, "I hate to ask it, but would you drive me back to the Snows' place?"

Chief Parsons looked at her sharply. "Don't you feel good, Increase?"

"Just a little strange," Mrs. Judbury said quietly.

"Sure. Nobody in this crowd will even miss us. Those Partridges sure have Haunt Port in the palm of their hands!"

Nearly an hour later in the beach house kitchen, Mrs. Judbury slammed the broom closet door shut. "And that's the secret staircase and that's the Witch's Hollow loot," she said to Chief Parsons. "Will you go along with Keith's plan?"

Chief Parsons rubbed his head. "My stars, Increase! You and that boy have been meddling with stolen property!"

Mrs. Judbury sighed. "Thaddeus Parsons, will you get your mind off what we've done and on to what you should *do?* Find out if there *is* such a ship as the *Turkish Rose.* And if there is, find out where she's bound right now. Then call the federal agents—or whoever you call in cases like this—and get them up here quick. And keep them *out of sight*."

Chief Parsons stepped out through the kitchen doorway. He shook his head. "Well, I've known you a long time and I'm going along with you in this. In fact, it's too late to do anything else. I'm not intending to arrest you for breaking and entering and moving stolen property. But I'll probably lose the fall election because of it."

Mrs. Judbury's black eyes twinkled. "You mean the newspaper headlines will say, 'Haunt Port Police Chief Under Spell of Local Witch'?"

"No," Chief Parsons answered gloomily. "I see something more like 'Haunt Port Police Chief Leads Gang of International Art Thieves.'"

For the first time in long, long years, Mrs. Judbury laughed—laughed hard.

"Before I'd let that happen, I'd . . . well, I'd say I'd *bewitched* you."

"No need," Chief Parsons said gruffly, stepping into his car. "And Increase—it was real nice to see you and Pru at the clambake."

KEITH TAKES COMMAND

☐ From his perch on the sun-warmed rocks, Keith Partridge stared gloomily out at the blue Atlantic. Today the ocean was as quiet and smooth as the cove.

He sighed and turned to Pru and Laurie, who were helpfully pouring suntan oil on each other's shoulders.

"Do you realize not a thing has happened since the Night of the Toads—and here it is, Tuesday. If it weren't for that stuff on the staircase, I'd think I'd dreamed the whole thing."

"That's all right with me!" Laurie exclaimed. "For a while there I thought we weren't ever going to get around to concentrating on vacation."

Pru laughed. "I've never had so much fun! Gosh! First the beach party last Thursday, and then the clambake Saturday night, then Mr. Kinkaid's taking us to dinner on Sunday before he left, and—"

"Jane's movie party last night," Laurie added.

"And *nothing* today—so far," Keith muttered.

"Well, it's only ten forty-five A.M." Laurie laughed. "Cheer up, Keith."

"Here come the kids," Pru said, looking up.

Chris, Danny, and Tracy began calling out their news as they scrambled and bounded down the rocks.

"Hey!" Chris shouted. "We have to pack up right away."

"We're leaving," Danny yelled. "This afternoon."

"And you and your mother are invited, Pru," Tracy puffed as she slid over the last rounded boulder. "Mr. Kinkaid said so."

Chris handed Keith a sheet of paper. "Here, Keith. Mom said Western Union phoned it, and she wrote it out."

Keith looked down at his mother's familiar handwriting and read aloud:

Hate to cut in on vacation but singing date too good to miss. May mean big contract later. Will explain. Take flight 509 from Boston to Portland at 3:00. Have closed office. Will meet you. Bring Judburys. Trip's on me. Can return to beach house tomorrow.

Reuben Kinkaid

Laurie jumped up. "My hair's a mess!" she exclaimed. "My gosh! I'd better get going."

"Keith, do you think Mr. Kinkaid means Portland, Oregon?" Danny asked. "Mom says Portland, Maine, but I'd like to see Oregon, and Mr. Kinkaid said the trip was on him."

Keith didn't answer. He was staring at the message as though he were hypnotized. Then suddenly he sprang to his feet, dashed up the rocks, leaving five surprised faces staring after him.

"I can't understand why Reuben wouldn't have discussed this over the phone," Shirley said as Keith came in. "All that packing and unpacking and all that *rush!* He just doesn't know the meaning of the word vacation."

Keith hardly stopped to listen. He strode to the telephone.

"If you're calling Jane Parsons," Shirley called after him, "tell her we'll drop the keys off at the grocery."

Keith didn't reply. He was already dialing Reuben Kinkaid's office number.

In a moment, he called out, "Mom! Hey, Mom! Reuben's on the phone. He wants to talk with you."

He handed over the telephone and dashed on out to the kitchen. "Mrs. Judbury!" he exclaimed. "*I* just got the signal, I think. Something's going to happen tonight. I'm sure of it. That message was a fake."

To his astonishment, Mrs. Judbury didn't look surprised. "I know," she said calmly, and kept right on snapping string beans into a saucepan.

"Then let's *do* something!" Keith exclaimed excitedly.

"Something's already being done," Mrs. Judbury replied. "Thaddeus Parsons called about an hour ago and told me the *Turkish Rose* would be putting into Boston early tomorrow morning. He figured that means she might be in these waters tonight. And I guess by now he's on his way to Boston to talk with the authorities there."

Keith stared. "I don't get it. What's the *Turkish Rose?*"

"It's a ship," Mrs. Judbury said. "Now, Keith, don't get your dander up. When I told you that Thaddeus had agreed to go along with your ESP kind of idea, I didn't tell you about my sort of seeing a ship with that name. Goodness knows I felt foolish enough telling Thaddeus about it."

Keith flushed angrily. "I thought we were together in this."

Mrs. Judbury nodded. "We are. And I was going to tell you as soon as there was something to tell. But then when Thaddeus called, you weren't here.

"Keith, if I'm right, nobody's coming to *get* the loot they think is in the cottage—but somebody is coming to bring *more in*. There probably will be a rendezvous at sea, then a small boat will come into the cove and unload."

"Man!" Keith breathed. "This *is* going to be something!"

Mrs. Judbury nodded. "You can't tell what kind of doings will be going on in that cove tonight. And that message was heaven-sent even though it was a fake. You'll all be safe in Portland tonight."

"Safe in *Portland!*"

Before he could say more, Shirley walked into the kitchen. "Keith," she asked, "how on earth did you happen to think of checking back on Reuben's wire? That message was a complete fake. He's absolutely dumbfounded. And so am I."

Mrs. Judbury groaned and Shirley turned to her. "Now, never mind, Mrs. Judbury," she said. "I know a trip would have been fun for you and Pru, but—. Now what? There goes that telephone again."

When Shirley left the kitchen, Mrs. Judbury looked at Keith. Her face was as red as a cranberry in a Massachusetts bog. "I've never felt so guilty in my life," she said. "Keith, what's your mother going to say when she finds out she's the only person outside of the children who doesn't know about the loot on the staircase? She'll be pretty mad, or I miss my guess. Keith, we *have* to tell her now."

But Shirley's next words when she came back into the kitchen knocked out any thought of confessing.

"The most awful thing has happened," she exclaimed. "Mrs. Parsons just had a call from a Boston hospital that Chief Parsons has been in an automobile accident. She doesn't know how badly he's hurt, and she's asked me to drive her and Jane into the city right away. Of course I said I would. It may mean we won't be back until late. What a day!"

She raced out of the kitchen and hurried upstairs to change her clothes.

Keith looked at Mrs. Judbury and she looked at Keith. "Now what?" Keith asked.

"Poor Thaddeus." Mrs. Judbury said worriedly. "I hope he hasn't been badly hurt."

"I'll ask Mom to call us from Boston as soon as they know," Keith said. "Maybe if it isn't serious, Jane can come to the phone and I can talk with her about whatever arrangements her dad made."

"Forget about any doings at Witch's Hollow tonight," Mrs. Judbury said.

"Forget it!" Keith exclaimed. "Heck, NO!"

"If you think you're going to capture—goodness knows who—singled handed, put it right out of your head," Mrs. Judbury said firmly.

Keith glared at her. "I'm not exactly Tracy's age, you know," he said hotly. "We can call the federal agents ourselves and find out if Chief Parsons made a plan with them."

"Oh?" Mrs. Judbury asked. "And which federal agents, pray tell? There are all kinds, or so I've heard. And you don't have the least notion who Thaddeus would have called, if he called at all."

Shirley came hurrying back down the stairs. "Keith, didn't you leave the motorboat at the Haunt Port wharf? I could drop you off there in case you want it today."

Instantly, an idea sprang into Keith's head. "Good idea. And maybe Pru will want to come along, too. She may want to use her sailboat."

As the three drove off in the station wagon, Laurie, her hair rolled in pink curlers, walked into the kitchen.

"Of all the times to shampoo my hair!" she said. "Just when I could have been helping and going with Mom to Boston."

"Well, I daresay it's best that you're here," Mrs. Judbury said. "Why don't you get on the phone and call Bailey Parsons? He and Bill must be stranded, with the Parsons away. Tell them to hurry down to the wharf and come back here with Keith and Pru on the boat."

"Oh!" Laurie rushed off. "I hope I can catch them!"

Mrs. Judbury sighed. "Thank goodness I thought of that," she said to herself. "Now the kids can have a rock session tonight right here in the *house*. And I'll be on the job in the cove."

Unluckily, Mrs. Judbury's ESP seemed to be out of order.

At that moment, Pru and Keith were at Pru's house, carefully wrapping Mr. Judbury's old deer rifle in a faded patchwork quilt.

"There's no ammunition for it," Pru said.

"That's okay," Keith answered. "Come on. Let's hurry. I want to be home if Mom calls. Maybe I can talk with Jane—that is, if her dad is okay."

"You like Jane pretty much, don't you?" Pru asked.

Keith frowned. "Man!" he thought. "Don't girls ever think of anything besides romance?"

PRU'S TRIAL BY WATER

☐ Just as Mrs. Judbury was taking the roast from the oven and Laurie and Pru were filling a platter with steaming ears of corn, Mr. Beresford's car came gliding to a stop at the kitchen door.

Laurie looked up. "Oh! It's Mr. Beresford!" she exclaimed. Hastily putting down the tongs she had been using, she went to the kitchen doorway.

Mr. Beresford, cap in hand, smiled. "Excuse me for calling just at your dinner hour," he said, "but I heard in the village that your mother had gone up to Boston with Mrs. Parsons and Jane."

Laurie smiled. "It's *good* news, Mr. Beresford. Mother called us and said he is going to be released tomorrow, so she's staying over to drive them home in the morning."

"Then I guess with good news like that you'll be having another party in the cove to celebrate, won't you?" Mr. Beresford asked silkily.

Laurie laughed. "Well, you've almost guessed it. It's a party all right. Nobody's missing but Jane. And she talked with Keith and said she'll be with us in spirit. But we're going to stay up here. There's no electricity down in the cove, you know, and Keith can't use his electric guitar down there. I hope our rock session won't bother you."

Mr. Beresford smiled. "Not at all, my dear. In fact, I might enjoy hearing you young people all up here having a good time."

"Drop in," Laurie urged, "if you'd like to."

Mr. Beresford touched his cap. "Thank you. And my best to the Parsons when you see them. I'll be on my way now."

Laurie watched him drive away. She sighed. "Of all the men I've ever met, he's absolutely the most—most *elegant*," she thought. "Keith is *so* unfair about him."

At 9:30, Mrs. Judbury, sitting at the kitchen table, tried to read a book. "I just can't concentrate with that racket going on," she thought. "But thank goodness! It's keeping them busy."

She glanced at the kitchen clock. The hands pointed to 9:45. "Another fifteen minutes and I'll go down to the cove."

As she looked away from the clock, the shine of car headlights caught her eye. Her heart sank. "Maybe Mrs. Partridge has changed her mind and come home."

But it was Mr. Beresford again who came to the door.

"Good evening," he said. "Laurie was kind enough to invite me to drop in."

Mrs. Judbury opened the door. "I was just going to drop out, myself," she said. "I'll just never like rock music this close up, I guess. Come in."

Mr. Beresford followed her from the kitchen to the porch.

Nobody was there! The record player was churning out a great number, but not a soul was there, either playing or listening.

Mrs. Judbury paled. "Great heavens!" she exclaimed. She snapped off the booming music. Muscles along Mr. Beresford's jaw tightened. "Looks like you're not such a good baby-sitter, Mrs. Judbury," he said unpleasantly.

She turned and looked into his dark eyes—and it was like suddenly looking into two blazing hot evil furnaces. Suddenly she knew what she must do. Her thoughts raced madly.

"Now if those children aren't the ones!" she exclaimed. "But I'm half glad they're not here—it gives me a chance to consult you."

"Oh? About what?" Mr. Beresford asked suspiciously.

"You're an art collector, aren't you?" Mrs. Judbury asked in a strangely timid voice.

"Why do you ask?" Mr. Beresford said coldly.

Mrs. Judbury looked down at the floor. "Well, I don't know as I should say it—but, Mr. Beresford, Mrs. Snow must be an art collector, too. And I must say, I *wonder* about it. Follow me. I'll show you."

Mr. Beresford hesitated, then followed Mrs. Judbury as she strode back to the kitchen.

Swiftly, she opened the broom closet and emptied the mops, brooms, pails, and other clutter. "Now, Mr. Beresford, just step in here and *push*. Push that back wall."

Obligingly, Mr. Beresford pushed, and as the wall

swung in, Mrs. Judbury said, "You'll have to go in a step or two to see what I mean."

As Mr. Beresford stepped forward, Mrs. Judbury pushed hard against his back. He crashed across the steps in a terrible clatter of falling metal and thumping crates.

Swiftly, Mrs. Judbury pulled the door firmly shut. It locked in place. "Don't move around too much," she yelled. "You don't want to use up all the oxygen. You'll smother!"

Then calmly she replaced the contents of the broom closet and slammed the outer door.

"Heaven help me if I'm wrong," she told herself. "I wouldn't want to smother the wrong person. Now where are those kids?"

According to plan, "the kids" were at action stations Keith had assigned to each one.

It wasn't until after the children were in bed for the night and Mrs. Judbury was in the kitchen out of earshot that Keith had told the others what Jane really had meant when she said she'd "be with them in spirit."

Jane had talked with the FBI agents herself, and four men would be at the beach house between nine and nine-thirty.

But when nine-thirty came and went and no agents had appeared, Keith had speedily gone into action.

Now Laurie was stationed on the beach house side of the rock path leading to the cove. It was her job to guide the FBI men down the path when they arrived, and to sooth Mrs. Judbury's feathers.

In the light flung out from the kitchen door, she

had seen Mr. Beresford drive up, then go into the house. "My gosh," she groaned. "Now Mrs. Judbury will find out we're not there. Maybe I should warn Keith."

But instead, she waited and watched. "That's funny," she thought, puzzled. "Why doesn't he come out?"

Down in the cove, Keith, Bailey, and Bill each had picked hiding places behind the rocks. Keith, armed with the unloaded deer rifle, had taken the center position opposite the cottage doorway.

Only Pru was really uncomfortable. She huddled, wet and shivering, on the bottom of her little sailboat anchored out in the cove. The old patchwork quilt she had tucked around her was almost as wet as her bikini. Every now and then she raised her head and looked seaward. It was to be her job to swim over and cut the anchor rope if a smuggler's boat did anchor in the cove. The boat would then drift off toward Haunt Port, and a sea escape would be impossible.

In the dark star-pointed night, Keith was beginning to worry. "Maybe Jane didn't get the call through," he worried. "Maybe the FBI men missed the turnoff and aren't anywhere near here."

Suddenly, the cold barrel of the empty deer rifle seemed to be a silly idea. And now Bill and Bailey were involved, too. "What if something goes wrong?" Keith thought. "What if nothing happens? What if someone gets hurt?"

"Hey, Bailey! Bill!" he called softly. "Do you want to call it off?"

"Not now, I don't," Bill called back in a low voice. "We can't leave Pru. Look!"

Keith looked seaward. Against the black sky he saw the swiftly approaching running lights of a boat. As he watched, the sound of powerful engines of a fast launch reached his ears.

"Bailey," Keith called softly again, "get back to the beach house. Tell Mrs. Judbury to call police from *somewhere*."

But Mrs. Judbury wasn't in the house. She was striding along to the cove, five FBI agents trailing close behind.

Laurie scrambled down the path to give the word—to everybody but Pru!

It was too late for the FBI men to clear the cove of amateurs. Absolute silence was necessary.

"Every one of you duck behind a rock," the leader whispered sternly. "And no noise—and no *looking*. Stay down!"

Everything would have gone wonderfully if it hadn't been for Pru Judbury.

In the dead blackness along the cove, Pru couldn't see what was going on. And she certainly couldn't know FBI help had arrived. But in the dim starlight over the water, she *could* see a powerful launch glide to a stop out from shore. And she *could* hear the *plop* of an anchor dropped over the side.

Peering over the low gunwale of the little boat, Pru saw two men lower themselves waist-deep into the waters of the cove. A third man in the launch seemed to be lowering boxes over the side.

Then the rough, low voice of the man in the launch plainly reached her ears. "I'll take this last one myself, mates. We can make one trip of it tonight."

Pru heard the splash as the third man entered the water. She thought rapidly. "While they're sloshing around, they're less likely to hear me. Here goes."

Quickly, she rolled over the side and scooted in a silent sidestroke to the launch. She felt for the anchor rope and found it. "Thank goodness! It's rope and not cable!" she said to herself.

Even so, she had to saw hard back and forth to cut the strong nylon, and as the blade cut through, she immediately felt the drift carry the launch, not toward Haunt Port, but straight to the shore.

At that second, a gunshot rang out over the water and the sounds of thuds, scuffling, and men's heavy voices. Pru froze with fear. "That deer rifle wasn't loaded! What's happened to the kids? What have those men done to them?"

And while on the dark shore the smugglers were being securely handcuffed, Pru suddenly knew what she had to do.

She struck out quietly along the length of the drifting launch and felt for the rope ladder she was sure would be hanging over the side.

To a girl brought up in Haunt Port, Massachusetts, there was nothing new and strange about boats. Swiftly, she climbed aboard and went straight to the controls. "They'll never get away by sea," she whispered fiercely. "Not in this boat. Not *ever!*"

Her hand went to the starting switch. Instantly, the powerful engines revved into action and the big launch moved straight for the shore.

Wildly, Pru swung at the wheel. The launch, gaining speed, began a great curve out into the cove.

Lost in the roar of the engines, a voice shouted,

"Stop!" and a second shot sounded—this time aimed toward the water.

Pru, already well out into the cove, began to steady the wheel for a straight course to the open sea. To her horror it wouldn't budge. The steering mechanism had jammed. Now the launch began an ever-widening circle back toward shore.

"You've winged him," the FBI man shouted, as the launch went thundering past the shoreline. "He's going in circles!"

There was a harsh laugh from one of the three handcuffed men. "You've winged a ghost," he said. "*We're* all here."

It was Laurie who first realized what must have happened. "Pru!" she shrieked. "It's Pru!"

"*Prudence?*" Mrs. Judbury exclaimed. "What's Prudence doing out there?" she asked, horrified.

"Who's Prudence?" the leader of the FBI agents asked.

"My daughter," Mrs. Judbury answered, managing to keep her voice steady.

"*On that boat?*" The agent's voice was filled with shock. Then he yelled at the crowd. "Get up to the high rocks. *Move!* That boat will hit on its next pass!"

Keith alone ignored the warning. He ran to the very edge of the water as the launch came foaming and roaring, this time within fifteen feet of the shallows. "Pru!" he screamed with all the force of his lungs. "*Jump!* Hit the deep water!"

Then he, too, raced up the path to stand with the others and watch, horrified, as the launch made a last sickening giant swing out in the cove and back.

And none too soon. On the next thundering sweep,

the launch at full speed piled up on the rocks, and there was an explosive burst as the gasoline engines sent torches of flame into the sky.

Mrs. Judbury screamed. "This accursed place!" she cried. "Prudence! Prudence!"

Spark showers landed on the tinder-dry roof of Witch's Hollow, and as though in answer to Mrs. Judbury's cry, the old shingles hissed into flame.

Cove waters glowed red with fiery light.

"Look! Look!" Laurie pointed offshore. "It's Pru! She's safe!"

But Keith Partridge was taking no chances. Neither was Bill Angelo. Both boys leaped down the path and plunged into the water. In strong overhand strokes they reached Pru Judbury and brought her safely home.

Weakly, Mrs. Judbury sat down on a rock.

"It's all right, ma'am," an FBI agent said in a kind voice. "Your daughter is safe. But that cottage is sure a goner. Too bad!"

Mrs. Judbury seemed to come back to life. She jumped up. "Too *bad!*" she sang out. "Too *good!*"

Then her voice quieted. "Now I wonder why that girl never thought to cut back on the throttle?" she said crossly.

THE PARTRIDGE ESP

☐ Car headlights were beginning to stream along the drive as Mrs. Judbury led the way back to the beach house.

At least half of Haunt Port's citizens, coming to investigate an explosion and fire at Witch's Hollow, saw a parade instead, with Mrs. Judbury leading the march.

Behind her came Pru in a soaking wet bikini, her long hair straggling down like black satin seaweed.

Next in line of march were Laurie Partridge and Bailey Parsons lugging a narrow wooden crate between hem.

Keith Partridge and Bill Angelo, dripping wet, followed with another heavy box, and in back of them came eight men—three of them in handcuffs.

"You'll have to make a speech," Mrs. Judbury called back to the FBI leader. "Looks to me as though there's no getting out of here until that drive is cleared of cars."

All but one FBI man went straight into the beach house. He remained outside only long enough to announce that suspected smugglers had been captured, that the fire endangered no trees and would burn itself out, and would everybody please go home.

"Chief Parsons will be back tomorrow and will announce all available information at that time. Thank you for your interest," he said, then went into the house.

Inside the beach house, Simone was going wild with excitement. She dashed gaily around making everybody welcome—including the captives.

"Ma'am," the FBI spokesman said, "I'm leaving one of my men to get the details of the story at this end, and to stand guard on those boxes."

Mrs. Judbury's jaw dropped. She slapped a hand to her forehead. "For land's sake! There's a sight more to guard than *those!* Come!" she commanded, and went sailing off to the kitchen.

Even Simone was on hand to see Mr. Beresford come out from the secret staircase, spluttering, gasping, and furious.

Poor Simone took one look and let out a terrified *yipe*, and dashed under the kitchen table. And that was all Laurie Partridge needed. The stunned expression left her face and she stepped straight up to the once elegant Mr. Beresford.

"You—*you!* You stole Simone. You big . . . big lummox!"

"Lummox! I got another word for you," exclaimed one handcuffed captive. "Some brain you turned out to be!"

"You big dummy-builder!" Keith exploded.

"You *toad!*" Pru exclaimed.

The FBI men stared in amazement. "What goes on here?"

"You'll see," Mrs. Judbury said calmly. "Hold that man! And Keith, you get the flashlight and that painting in my room. There's quite a view in store for the FBI."

As things turned out, it was Laurie Partridge who solved the problem of how four agents and four prisoners were to return to Boston in one car.

"Why don't you borrow the Partridge Family bus?" she said generously. "We're not using it just now."

Dry clothes, hot chocolate, and Keith's guitar! A great windup for the night. But one thing was wrong —Keith strummed only one chord and stopped.

"What's wrong, Keith?" Laurie asked, as a strange expression came over her brother's face.

"It's my ESP," Keith groaned. "I'm getting a message."

Everybody stared at him.

He closed his eyes. "It's coming through *strong*. It's from somebody named—yes. Shirley Partridge, I think. Yep! It's Mom all right. The kids are with her, and she's saying, WHAT'S THE IDEA LEAVING US OUT OF ALL THE *FUN*?"